As You Like It
皆 大 欢 喜

[英]威廉·莎士比亚/著　朱生豪/译

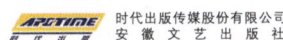
时代出版传媒股份有限公司
安 徽 文 艺 出 版 社

图书在版编目（CIP）数据

皆大欢喜/（英）威廉·莎士比亚（William Shakespeare）著；朱生豪译.—合肥：安徽文艺出版社，2019.2（2021.3 重印）

（莎士比亚戏剧典藏）

ISBN 978-7-5396-6148-3

Ⅰ.①皆… Ⅱ.①威… ②朱… Ⅲ.①喜剧－剧本－英国－中世纪 Ⅳ.①I561.33

中国版本图书馆 CIP 数据核字（2017）第 173818 号

出 版 人：段晓静
选题策划：姜婧婧　原典纪　　　统筹策划：刘　畅
责任编辑：姜婧婧　柯　谐　　　装帧设计：张诚鑫

出版发行：时代出版传媒股份有限公司　www.press-mart.com
　　　　　安徽文艺出版社　www.awpub.com
地　　址：合肥市翡翠路 1118 号　邮政编码：230071
营 销 部：(0551)63533889
印　　制：安徽新华印刷股份有限公司　(0551)65859551

开本：787×1092　1/32　印张：9.375　字数：220 千字
版次：2019 年 2 月第 1 版　2021 年 3 月第 2 次印刷
定价：42.00 元（精装）

（如发现印装质量问题，影响阅读，请与出版社联系调换）

版权所有，侵权必究

剧中人物

公爵	在放逐中
弗莱德里克	其弟,篡位者
阿米恩斯	流亡公爵的从臣
杰奎斯	流亡公爵的从臣
勒·波	弗莱德里克的侍臣
查尔斯	拳师
奥列佛	罗兰·德·鲍埃爵士的儿子
贾奎斯	罗兰·德·鲍埃爵士的儿子
奥兰多	罗兰·德·鲍埃爵士的儿子
亚当	奥列佛的仆人
丹尼斯	奥列佛的仆人
试金石	小丑
奥列佛·马坦克斯特师傅	牧师
柯林	牧人
西尔维斯	牧人
威廉	乡人,恋奥德蕾
扮许门者	
罗瑟琳	流亡公爵的女儿
西莉娅	弗莱德里克的女儿
菲苾	牧女
奥德蕾	村姑

众臣、侍童、林居人及侍从等

地点

奥列佛宅旁庭园；篡位者的宫廷；亚登森林

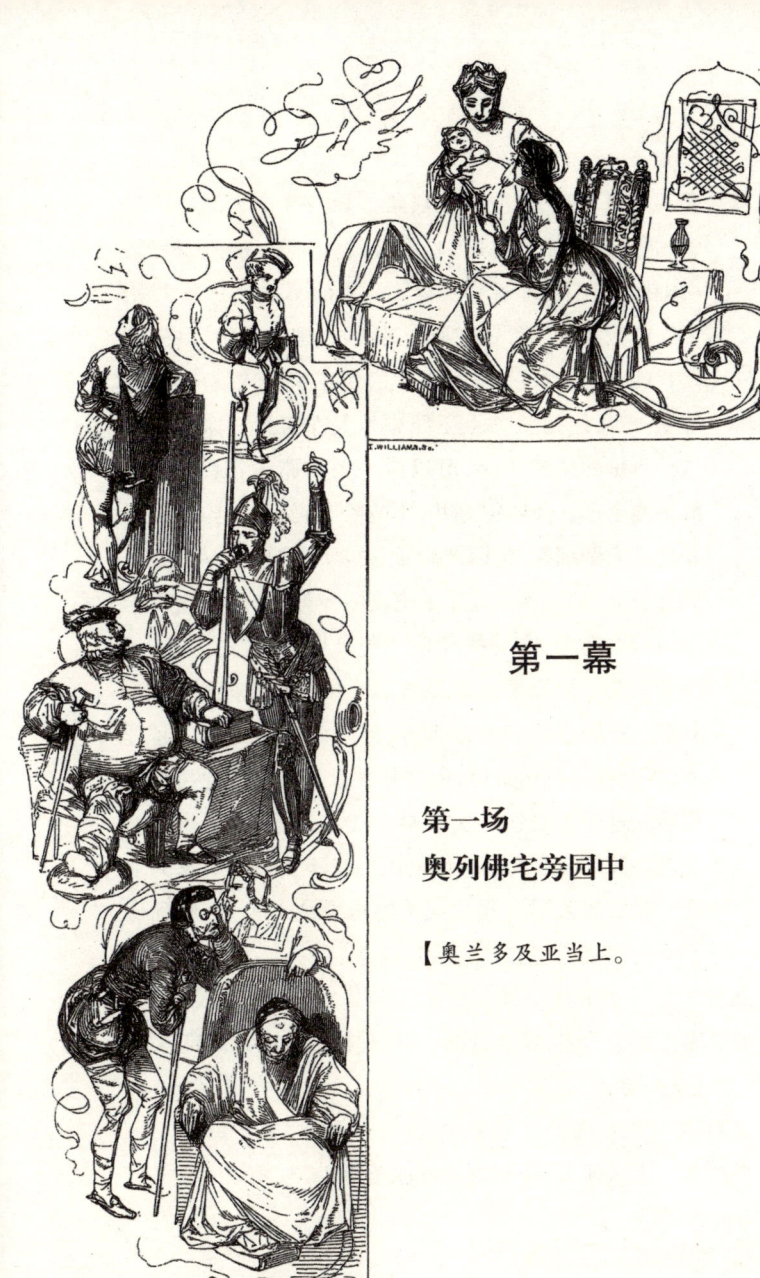

第一幕

第一场
奥列佛宅旁园中

【奥兰多及亚当上。

奥兰多　亚当,我记得遗嘱上只给了我一笔小小的一千块钱,而且正像你所说的,吩咐我的大哥把我好生教养,否则他不能得到他的祝福——我的不幸就这样开始了。他把我的二哥贾奎斯送进学校,据说成绩很好;可是我呢,他却叫我像个村汉似的住在家里,或者再说得确切一点,他把我一点不照顾地关在家里。你说像我这种身份的良家子弟,可以像一条牛那样养着吗?他的马匹也还比我养得好些,因为除了食料充足之外,还要把它们调练起来,因此用重金雇下了骑师。可是我,他的兄弟,却不曾在他手下得到一点好处,除了让我徒然地长大起来,这是我跟他那些粪堆上的畜生一样要感激他的。他除了这样慷慨地不给我什么之外,还要剥夺去我固有的一点点天分;他叫我和佃工在一起过活,不把我当兄弟看待,用这种教育来摧毁我的高贵的素质。这是使我伤心的缘故,亚当。我觉得在我身体之内的我的父亲的精神已经因为受不住这种奴隶的生活而反抗起来了。我一定不能再忍受下去,虽然我还不承想到避免它的妥当的方法。

亚当　大爷,您的哥哥从那边来了。

奥兰多　到旁边去,亚当,你就会听到他会怎样欺侮我。

【奥列佛上。

奥列佛　嘿,少爷!你来做什么?

奥兰多　不做什么,我不曾学习过做什么。

奥列佛　那么你在作践些什么呢,少爷?

奥兰多　哼,大爷,我在帮您的忙,把一个上帝造下来的、您的可怜的没有用处的兄弟用游荡来作践着哩。

奥列佛　那么你给我做事去,别站在这儿吧,少爷。

奥兰多　我要去看守您的猪,跟它们一起吃糠吗?我浪费什么了,才要受这种惩罚?

奥列佛　你知道你在什么地方吗,少爷?

奥兰多　噢,大爷,我知道得很清楚,我是在您的园子里。

奥列佛　你知道你是当着谁说话的吗,少爷?

奥兰多　噢,我知道我所当面的人,比他知道我要明白些。我知道你是我的大哥,照你的高贵的血统说起来,你也应该知道我是谁。按着世间的常礼,你的身份比我高些,因为你是长子;可是同样的礼法却不能取代我的血统,即使我们之间还有二十个兄弟。我的血液里有着跟你一样多的我们父亲的素质。虽然我承认你的居长在名分上是该格外受人敬重一些。

奥列佛　什么,孩子!

奥兰多　算了吧,算了吧,大哥,你不用这样卖老啊。

奥列佛　你要向我动起手来了吗,浑蛋?

奥兰多　我不是浑蛋,我是罗兰·德·鲍埃爵士的小儿子,他是我的父亲。谁敢说这样一位父亲会生下浑蛋儿子来的,才是个大浑蛋。你倘若不是我的哥哥,我这手一定不放松你的喉咙,直等我那另一只手拔出了你的舌头为止,因为你说了这样的话。你骂的是你自己。

亚当 （上前）好爷爷们,别生气;看在去世老爷的面子上,大家和和气气的吧!

奥列佛 放开我!

奥兰多 等我高兴放你的时候再放你。你一定要听我说话,父亲在遗嘱上吩咐你给我好好的教育,你却把我训练得像一个农夫,不让我跟上流社会接触。父亲的精神在我心中炽烈燃烧,我再也忍受不下去了。你得允许我去学习那种适合上流人身份的技艺,否则把父亲在遗嘱里指定给我的那笔小小的钱给了我,也好让我去自寻生路。

奥列佛 等到那笔钱用完了你便怎样?去做叫花子吗?哼,少爷,给我进去吧,别再给我找麻烦了。你可以得到你所要的一部分。请你走吧。

奥兰多 我不愿过分冒犯你,除了为我自身的利益。

奥列佛 你跟着他去吧,你这老狗!

亚当 "老狗"便是您给我的谢意吗?一点不错,我服侍您已经服侍得牙齿都落光了。上帝和我的老爷同在!他是绝不会说出这种话来的。(奥兰多、亚当下)

奥列佛 竟有这种事吗?你不服我管了吗?我要把你的傲气去掉,还不给你那一千块钱。喂,丹尼斯!

【丹尼斯上。

丹尼斯 大爷叫我吗?

奥列佛 公爵手下那个拳师查尔斯不是在这儿要跟我说话吗?

丹尼斯 禀大爷,他就在门口,要求见您哪。

奥列佛 叫他进来。(丹尼斯下)这是一个妙计。明天就是摔跤的日子。

【查尔斯上。

查尔斯 早安,大爷!

奥列佛 查尔斯好朋友,新朝廷里有些什么新消息?

查尔斯 朝廷里没有什么新消息,大爷,只有一些老消息:那就是说老公爵被他的弟弟新公爵放逐了;三四个忠心的大臣自愿跟着他出亡,他们的地产收入都给新公爵没收了去,因此他巴不得他们一个个滚蛋。

奥列佛 你知道公爵的女儿罗瑟琳是不是也跟她的父亲一起被放逐了?

查尔斯 啊,不,因为新公爵的女儿,她的族妹,自小便跟她在一个摇篮里长大,非常爱她,一定要跟她一同出亡,否则便要寻死。所以她现在仍旧在宫里,她的叔父把她像自家女儿一样看待着。从来不曾有两位小姐像她们这样要好了。

奥列佛 老公爵预备住在什么地方呢?

查尔斯　据说他已经住在亚登森林①,有好多人跟着他。他们在那边过着英国罗宾汉②那样的生活。据说每天有许多年轻贵人投奔到他那儿去,逍遥地把时间消磨过去,像是置身在古昔的黄金时代里一样。

奥列佛　喂,你明天要在新公爵面前摔跤吗?

查尔斯　正是,大爷。我来就是要通知您一件事情。我得到了一个风声,大爷,说您的弟弟奥兰多想要假扮了明天来跟我交手一下。明天这一场摔跤,大爷,是与我的名誉有关的,谁想不断一根骨头而安然逃出,必须好好留点儿神才行。令弟年纪太轻,顾念着咱们的交情,我不能下手把他打败;可是为了我自己的名誉起见,他如果要来,我却非得给他一点厉害不可。为此,看在咱们交情的分上,我特地来通报您一声:您或者劝他打消了这个念头;或者请您不要为了他所将要遭到的羞辱而生气,这全然是他自取其咎,并非我的本意。

奥列佛　查尔斯,多谢你对我的好意,我一定会重重报答你的。我自己也已经注意到舍弟的意思,曾经用婉言劝阻过他;可是他执意不改。我告诉你,查尔斯,他是在全法国顶不理可喻的一个兄弟,野心勃勃,一见人家有

---

①　亚登森林在法国与比利时的东北部,即 Forest of Ardennes;但莎翁意中所写的亚登森林,则为英国 Warwickshire 的 Forest of Arden。
②　罗宾汉(Robin Hood),英国传说中十四世纪时的著名侠盗。

什么好处,心里总是不服,而且老是在阴谋设计陷害我——他的同胞的兄长。一切悉听你的尊意吧,我巴不得你把他的头颈和手指一起揿断了呢。你得留心一些,要是你略为削了他一点面子,或者他不能大大地削你的面子,他就会用毒药毒死你,用奸谋陷害你,非把你的性命用卑鄙的手段除掉了才肯甘休。不瞒你说,我一说起也忍不住要流泪,在现在世界上没有比他更奸恶的年轻人了。为了自己兄弟的关系,我还不好怎样说他。假如我把他的真相完全告诉你,那我一定会因惭愧而哭泣,你也要脸色发白而大吃一惊的。

查尔斯　我真幸运上您这儿来。假如他明天来,我一定要给他一顿教训;倘若不叫他瘸了腿,我以后再不跟人家摔跤赌锦标了。好,上帝保佑您,大爷!(下)

奥列佛　再见,好查尔斯。——现在我要去挑拨这位好勇斗狠的家伙了。我希望他送了命。我自己也不明白为什么我是那么恨他。说起来他很善良,从来不曾受过教育,然而却很有学问,充满了高贵的思想,无论哪一等人都爱戴他,真的,大家都是这样喜欢他,尤其是我自己手下的人,以至于我倒给人家轻视起来。可是情形不会长久这样;这个拳师可以给我解决一切。现在我只消把那孩子激将前去就是了。我就去。(下)

第二场
公爵宫门前草地

【罗瑟琳及西莉娅上。

西莉娅　罗瑟琳,我的好姊姊,请你快活些吧。

罗瑟琳　亲爱的西莉娅,我已经强作欢容,你还要我再快活一些吗?除非你能够教我怎样忘掉一个被放逐的父亲,否则你总不能叫我想起无论怎样有趣的事情。

西莉娅　我看出你爱我抵不上我爱你那样深。要是我的伯父,你被放逐的父亲,放逐了你的叔父,我的父亲,只要你仍旧跟我在一起,我可以爱你的父亲就像我自己的父亲一样。假如你爱我也像我爱你一样真纯,那么你也一定会这样的。

罗瑟琳 好,我愿意忘记我自己的处境,为了你而高兴起来。

西莉娅 你知道我父亲只有我一个孩子,看来也不见得会再有了,等他去世之后,你便可以承继他,因为凡是他用暴力从你父亲手里夺了来的,我便要用爱心归还给你。凭着我的名誉起誓,我一定会这样;要是我背了誓,让我变成个妖怪。所以,我的好罗瑟琳,我的亲爱的罗瑟琳,快活起来吧。

罗瑟琳 妹妹,从此以后我要高兴起来,想出一些消遣的法子。让我看,你觉得来一下子恋爱怎样?

西莉娅 好的,不妨作为消遣,可是不要认真爱起人来;而且玩笑也总不要开得过度,羞答答地脸红了一下子就算了,不要弄到丢了脸摆不脱身。

罗瑟琳 那么我们作什么消遣呢?

西莉娅 让我们坐下来嘲笑那位好管家太太命运之神,叫她羞得离开了纺车,免得她的赏赐老是不公平①。

---

① 命运女神于纺车上织人类的命运,因命运赏罚毫无定准,故下文云"瞎眼婆子"。

罗瑟琳 我希望我们能够这样做,因为她的恩典完全是滥给的。这位慷慨的瞎眼婆子在给女人赏赐的时候尤其是乱来。

西莉娅 一点不错,因为被她给了美貌的,她总不让她们贞洁;被她给了贞洁的,她便叫她们生得怪难看的。

罗瑟琳 不,现在你把命运的职务拉扯到造物身上去了;命运管理着人间的赏罚,可是管不了天生的相貌。

【试金石上。

西莉娅 管不了吗?造物生下了一个美貌的人儿来,命运不会把她推到火里去从而毁坏她的容颜吗?造物虽然给我们智慧,可以把命运取笑,可是命运不已经差这个傻瓜来打断我们的谈话了吗?

罗瑟琳 真的,那么命运太对不起造物了,她会叫一个天生的傻瓜来打断天生的智慧。

西莉娅 也许这也不干命运的事,而是造物的意思,因为看到我们天生的智慧太迟钝了,不配议论神明,所以才叫这傻瓜来做我们的砺石;因为傻瓜的愚蠢往往是聪明人的砺石。喂,聪明人!你到哪儿去?

试金石 小姐,快到您父亲那儿去。

西莉娅 你做起差人来了吗?

试金石 不,我以名誉为誓,我是奉命来请您去的。

罗瑟琳 傻瓜,你从哪儿学来的这一句誓?

试金石 从一个武士那儿学来,他以名誉为誓说煎饼很好,又以名誉为誓说芥末不行；可是我知道煎饼不行，芥末很好。然而那武士却也不曾发假誓。

西莉娅　你怎样用你那一大堆的学问证明他不曾发假誓呢？

罗瑟琳　噢，对了，请把你的聪明施展出来吧。

试金石　您二人都站出来，摸摸你们的下巴，以你们的胡须为誓说我是个坏蛋。

西莉娅　以我们的胡须为誓，要是我们有胡须的话，你是个坏蛋。

试金石　以我的坏蛋的身份为誓，要是我有坏蛋的身份的话，那么我便是个坏蛋。可是假如你们用你们所没有的东西起誓，你们便不算是发的假誓。这个武士用他的名誉起誓，因为他从来不曾有过什么名誉，所以他也不算是发假誓；即使他曾经有过名誉，也早已在他看见这些煎饼和芥末之前发誓发掉了。

西莉娅　请问你说的是谁？

试金石　是您的父亲老弗莱德里克所喜欢的一个人。

西莉娅　我的父亲欢喜他，他也就够有名誉的了。够了，别再说起他。你总有一天会因为把人讥诮而吃鞭子的。

试金石　这就可发一叹了，聪明人可以做傻事，傻子却不准说聪明话。

西莉娅　真的，你说得对。自从把傻子的一点点小聪明禁止发表之后，聪明人的一点点小小的傻气却大大地显起身手来了。——勒·波先生来啦。

罗瑟琳 含着满嘴的新闻。

西莉娅 他会把他的新闻向我们倾吐出来,就像鸽子哺雏一样。

罗瑟琳 那么我们要塞满一肚子的新闻了。

西莉娅 那再好不过了,塞得胖胖的,卖出去更值钱些。

【勒·波上。

西莉娅 您好,勒·波先生。有什么新闻?

勒·波 好郡主,您错过一场很好的玩意儿了。

西莉娅 玩意儿!什么花色的?

勒·波 什么花色的,小姐!我怎么回答您呢?

罗瑟琳 凭着您的聪明和您的机缘吧。

试金石 或者按照着命运女神的旨意。

西莉娅 说得好,极堆砌之能事了。

勒·波 两位小姐,你们叫我莫名其妙。我是要来告诉你们有一场很好的摔跤,你们错过机会了。

罗瑟琳 把那场摔跤的情形讲给我们听吧。

勒·波 我可以把开场的情形告诉你们。假如两位小姐听着乐意,收场的情形你们可以自己看一个明白,精彩的部分还不曾开始呢。他们就要到这儿来表演了。

西莉娅 好,就把那个已经陈旧了的开场说来听听。

勒·波 有一个老人带着他的三个儿子到来——

西莉娅 我可以把这开头接上一个老故事去。

勒·波　三个漂亮的青年,长得一表人才——

罗瑟琳　头颈里挂着招贴,"特此布告,俾众周知"。

勒·波　老大跟公爵的拳师查尔斯摔跤,查尔斯一下子就把他摔倒了,打断了三根肋骨,生命已无希望;老二、老三也都这样给他对付过去。他们都躺在那边。那个可怜的老头子,他们的父亲,在为他们痛哭,惹得旁观的人都陪他落泪。

罗瑟琳　哎哟!

试金石　但是,先生,您说小姐们错过了的玩意儿是什么呢?

勒·波　哪,就是我说过的这件事啊。

试金石　所以人们每天都可以增进一些见识。我今天才第一次听见折断肋骨是小姐们的玩意儿。

西莉娅　我也是第一次呢。

罗瑟琳　可是还有谁想要听自己肋下清脆动人的一声吗?还有谁喜欢让他的肋骨给人敲断吗?妹妹,我们要不要去看他们摔跤?

勒·波　要是你们不走开,那么不看也得看;因为这儿正是指定摔跤的地方,他们就要来表演了。

西莉娅　真的,他们从那边来了;让我们不要走开,看一下子吧。

【喇叭奏花腔。弗莱德里克公爵、众臣、奥兰多、查尔斯及侍从等上。

弗莱德里克 来吧。那年轻人既然不肯听劝,就让他吃些苦头,也是他自不量力的报应。

罗瑟琳 那边就是那个人吗?

勒·波 就是他,小姐。

西莉娅 唉!他太年轻啦;可是瞧上去倒好像很有得胜的神气。

弗莱德里克 啊,吾儿和侄女!你们也溜到这儿来看摔跤吗?

罗瑟琳 是的,殿下,请您准许我们。

弗莱德里克 我可以断定你们一定不会感到有趣的,两方的实力太不平均了。我因为可怜这个挑战的人年纪轻轻,想把他劝阻了,可是他不肯听劝。小姐们,你们去对他说说,看能不能说服他。

西莉娅 叫他过来,勒·波先生。

弗莱德里克 好吧,我就走开。(退至一旁)

勒·波 挑战的先生,两位郡主有请。

奥兰多 敢不从命。

罗瑟琳 年轻人,你向拳师查尔斯挑战了吗?

奥兰多 不,美貌的郡主,他才是向众人挑战的人;我不过像别人一样来到这儿,想要跟他较量较量我的青春的力量。

西莉娅 年轻的先生,照您的年纪而论,您的胆量是太大了。您已经看见了这个人的无情的蛮力。要是您能够用您的眼睛瞧见您自己的形状,或者用您的理智判断您自己的能力,那么您对于这回冒险所怀的戒惧,一定会劝您另外找一件比较适宜于您的事情来做。为了您自己的缘故,我们请求您顾虑您自身的安全,放弃了这种尝试吧。

罗瑟琳　是的,年轻的先生,您的名誉不会因此而受损;我们可以去请求公爵停止这场摔跤。

奥兰多　我要请你们原谅,我觉得我自己十分有罪,胆敢拒绝这么两位美貌出众的小姐的要求。可是让你们的美貌和好意伴送着我去做这场决斗吧。假如我打败了,那不过是一个从来不曾给人看重过的人丢了脸;假如我死了,也不过死了一个自己愿意寻死的人。我不会辜负我的朋友们,因为没有人会哀悼我;我不会对世间有什么损害,因为我在世上一无所有;我不过在世间占了一个位置,也许死后可以让更好的人来补充。

罗瑟琳　我但愿我所有的一点点微弱的气力也加在您身上。

西莉娅　我也愿意把我的气力再加在她的气力上面。

罗瑟琳　再会。求上天但愿我错看了您!

西莉娅　愿您的希望成全!

查尔斯　来,这个想要来送死的哥儿在什么地方?

奥兰多　已经预备好了,朋友,可是他却不像你这样傲慢。

弗莱德里克　你们斗一个回合就够了。

查尔斯 不,启禀殿下,您第一次已经敦劝过他,第二次就可以不必再劝他了。

奥兰多 你要在以后嘲笑我,可不必事先就嘲笑起来。来啊。

罗瑟琳 赫拉克勒斯默佑着你,年轻人!

西莉娅 我希望我有隐身术,去拉住那强徒的腿。(查尔斯、奥兰多二人摔跤)

罗瑟琳 啊,出色的青年!

西莉娅 假如我的眼睛里会打雷,我知道谁是要被打倒的。(查尔斯被摔倒;欢呼声)

弗莱德里克 算了,算了。

奥兰多 请殿下准许我再试,我的一口气还不曾透完哩。

弗莱德里克 你怎样啦,查尔斯?

勒·波 他说不出话来了,殿下。

弗莱德里克 把他抬出去。你叫什么名字,年轻人?(查尔斯被抬下)

奥兰多 禀殿下,我是奥兰多,罗兰·德·鲍埃的幼子。

弗莱德里克 我希望你是别人的儿子。世间都以为你的父亲是个好人,但他却是我永远的仇敌。假如你是别族的子孙,你今天的行事一定可以使我更喜欢你一些。再见吧。你是个勇敢的青年,我情愿你向我说起的是另外一个父亲。(弗莱德里克、勒·波及随从下)

西莉娅 姊姊,假如我处在我父亲的地位,我会做这种事吗?

奥兰多　我以做罗兰爵士的儿子为荣,即使只是他的幼子;我不愿改变我的地位,过继给弗莱德里克做后嗣。

罗瑟琳　我的父亲宠爱罗兰爵士,就像他的灵魂一样;全世界都抱着和我父亲同样的意见。要是我本来就已经知道这位青年便是他的儿子,我一定含着眼泪谏劝他不要做这种冒险。

西莉娅　好姊姊,让我们到他跟前去鼓励鼓励他。我父亲的无礼猜忌的脾气,使我十分痛心。——先生,您很值得尊敬;要是您在恋爱上也像在别的事情上一样守信,那么您的情人一定是很有福气的。

罗瑟琳　先生,(自颈上取下项链赠奥兰多)为了我的缘故,请戴上这个吧。我是个失爱于命运的人,心有余而力不足,不过略表微忱而已。我们去吧,妹妹。

西莉娅　好。再见,好先生。

奥兰多　我不能说一句谢谢您吗?我的勇气已丧失,站在这儿的只是一个人形的枪靶、一块没有生命的木石。

罗瑟琳　他在叫我们回去。我的矜傲随着我的命运一起摧毁了;我且去问他有什么话说。您叫我们吗,先生? 先生,您摔跤摔得很好;给您征服了的,不单是您的敌人。

西莉娅　去吧,姊姊。

罗瑟琳　你先走,我跟着你。再会。(罗瑟琳、西莉娅下)

奥兰多　什么一种情感重压住我的舌头?虽然她想跟我交

谈,我却想不出话来对她说。可怜的奥兰多啊,你给征服了!战胜了你的,不是查尔斯,却是比他更柔弱的人儿。

【勒·波重上。

勒·波　先生,我为着好意劝您还是离开这地方吧。虽然您很值得恭维、赞扬和敬爱,但是公爵的脾气太坏,他会把您一切的行事都误会了。公爵的心性有点捉摸不定;他的为人怎样我不便说,还是您自己去忖度忖度吧。

奥兰多　谢谢您,先生。我还要请您告诉我,这两位小姐中间哪一位是在场的公爵的女儿?

勒·波　要是我们照行为举止上看起来,两个可说都不是他的女儿;但是那位矮小一点的是他的女儿。另外一位便是放逐在外的公爵所生,被她这位篡位的叔父留在这儿陪伴他的女儿。她们两人的相爱是远过于同胞姊妹的。但是我可以告诉您,新近公爵对于他这位温柔的侄女有点不乐意,毫无理由,只是因为人民都称赞她的品德,为了她那位好父亲的缘故而同情她。我可以断定他对这位小姐的恶意不久就会突然显露出来。再会吧,先生。我希望在另外一个较好的世界里可以再跟您多多结识。

奥兰多　我非常感谢您的好意。再会。(勒·波下)才穿过浓烟,又钻进烈火;一边是专制的公爵,一边是暴虐的

哥哥。可是天仙一样的罗瑟琳啊!(下)

第三场
宫中一室

【西莉娅及罗瑟琳上。

西莉娅 喂,姊姊!喂,罗瑟琳!爱神哪!没有一句话吗?

罗瑟琳 连可以丢给一条狗的一句话也没有。

西莉娅 不,你的话是太宝贵了,怎么可以丢给贱狗呢?丢给我几句吧。来,讲一些道理来叫我浑身瘫痪。

罗瑟琳 那么姊妹两人都害了病了:一个是给道理害得浑

19

身瘫痪,一个是因为想不出什么道理来而发了疯。

西莉娅 但这是不是全然为了你的父亲?

罗瑟琳 不,一部分是为了我的孩子的父亲。唉,这个平凡的世间是多么荆棘遍布呀!

西莉娅 姊姊,这不过是些有刺的果壳,为了取笑玩玩而丢在你身上的。要是我们不在道上走,我们的裙子就要给它们抓住。

罗瑟琳 在衣裳上的,我可以把它们抖去;但是这些刺是在我的心里呢。

西莉娅 你咳嗽一声就咳出来了。

罗瑟琳 要是我咳嗽一声,他就会应声而来,那么我倒会试一下。

西莉娅 算了算了。使劲地把你的爱情克服下来吧。

罗瑟琳 唉!我的爱情比我气力大得多哩!

西莉娅 啊,那么我替你祝福吧!即使你要失败,也得试一下。但是把笑话搁在一旁,让我们正正经经地谈谈。你真的会突然这样猛烈地爱上老罗兰爵士的小儿子吗?

罗瑟琳 我的父亲和他的父亲非常要好呢。

西莉娅 因此你也必须和他的儿子非常要好吗?照这样说起来,那么我的父亲非常恨他的父亲,因此我也应当恨他了;可是我却不恨奥兰多。

罗瑟琳 不,看在我的面上,不要恨他。

西莉娅 为什么不呢?他不是值得恨的吗?

罗瑟琳 因为他是值得爱的,所以让我爱他;因为我爱他,所以你也要爱他。瞧,公爵来了。

西莉娅 他满眼都是怒气。

【弗莱德里克公爵率从臣上。

弗莱德里克 姑娘,为了你的安全,你得赶快收拾起来,离开我们的宫廷。

罗瑟琳 我吗,叔父?

弗莱德里克 你,侄女。在这十天之内,要是你被发现在离我们宫廷二十英里之内,你就得被处死。

罗瑟琳 请殿下开示我,我犯了什么罪过。要是我有自知之明,要是我并没有做梦,也不曾发疯——我相信我没有——那么,亲爱的叔父,我从来不曾起过半分触犯您老人家的念头。

弗莱德里克 一切叛徒都是这样的。要是他们凭着口头的话便可以免罪,那么他们都是再清白没有的了。可是我不能信任你,这一句话就够了。

罗瑟琳 但是您的不信任不能使我变成叛徒。请告诉我您有什么证据。

弗莱德里克 你是你父亲的女儿。还用得着说别的话吗?

罗瑟琳 当殿下您夺去了我父亲的公国的时候,我就是他的女儿;当殿下您把他放逐的时候,我也还是他的女儿。叛逆并不是遗传的,殿下。即使我们受到亲友的牵连,那与我又有什么相干?我的父亲并不是个叛徒呀。所以,殿下,别看错了我,把我的窘迫看作了奸慝。
西莉娅 好殿下,听我说。
弗莱德里克 嗯,西莉娅,我让她留在这儿,只是为了你的缘故,否则她早已跟她的父亲流浪去了。
西莉娅 那时我没有请您让她留下;那是您自己的主意,因为您自己觉得不好意思。那时我还太小,不曾知道她的好处;但现在我知道了。要是她是个叛逆,那么我也是。我们一直都睡在一起,同时起床,一块儿读书,同游同食,无论到什么地方去,都像朱诺的一双天鹅①,永远成着对,拆不开来。
弗莱德里克 她这人太阴险,你敌不过她。她的和气、她的沉默和她的忍耐,都能感动人心,叫人民可怜她。你是个傻子,她已经夺去了你的名誉;她去了之后,你就可以显得格外光彩而贤德了。所以闭住你的嘴,我对她所下的判决是确定而无可挽回的,她必须被放逐。
西莉娅 那么您把这句判决也加在我身上吧,殿下;我没有她做伴便活不下去。
弗莱德里克 你是个傻子。侄女,你得准备起来,假如误了期限,凭着我的名誉和我的言出如山的命令,要把你处死。(偕从臣下)

---

① 按:朱诺(Juno,天后)之鸟为孔雀,天鹅为维纳斯(Uenus,爱神)之鸟。

西莉娅　唉,我的可怜的罗瑟琳!你到哪儿去呢?你肯不肯换一个父亲?我把我的父亲给了你吧。请你不要比我更伤心。

罗瑟琳　我比你有更多的伤心的理由。

西莉娅　你没有,姊姊。请你高兴一点。你知道不知道,公爵把他的女儿也放逐了?

罗瑟琳　他没有。

西莉娅　没有?那么罗瑟琳还没有那种爱情,使你明白你我二人有如一体。我们难道要被拆散了吗?我们难道要分手了吗,亲爱的姑娘?不,让我的父亲另外找一个后嗣吧。你应该跟我商量我们应当怎样飞走,到哪儿去,带些什么东西。不要因为环境的变迁而独自伤心,让我分担一些你的心事吧。我对着因为同情我们而惨白的天空起誓,无论你怎样说,我都要跟你一起走。

罗瑟琳　但是我们到哪儿去呢?

西莉娅　到亚登森林找我的伯父去。

罗瑟琳　唉,像我们这样的姑娘家,走这么远路,该是多么危险!美貌比金银更容易引起盗心呢。

西莉娅　我可以穿了破旧的衣裳,用些黄泥涂在脸上,你也这样,我们便可以通行过去,不会遭人家算计了。

罗瑟琳　我的身材特别高,完全穿得像个男人岂不更好?腰间插一把出色的匕首,手里拿一柄刺野猪的长矛;心里尽管隐藏着女人家的胆怯,但要在外表上装出一副雄赳起气昂昂的样子来，正像那些冒充好汉的懦夫一般。

西莉娅 你做了男人之后，我叫你什么名字呢？

罗瑟琳 我要取一个和乔武的侍童一样的名字，所以你叫我盖尼米德①吧。但是你叫什么呢？

西莉娅 我要取一个可以表示我的境况的名字。我不再叫西莉娅，就叫爱莲娜②吧。

罗瑟琳 但是妹妹，我们设法去把你父亲宫廷里的小丑偷来好不好？他在我们的旅途中不是可以给我们解闷吗？

西莉娅 他要跟着我走遍广大的世界；让我独自去对他说吧。我们且去把珠宝钱物收拾起来。我出走之后，他们一定要追寻，我们该想出一个顶适当的时间和顶安全的方法来避过他们。现在我们是满心的欢畅，去找寻自由，不是流亡。（同下）

① 盖尼米德（Ganymede），乔武（Jove，即 Jupiter）之持爵童子。
② 爱莲娜，原文 Aliena，暗示 alienated（远隔）之意。

第二幕

第一场
亚登森林

【老公爵、阿米恩斯及众臣做林居人装束上。

公爵　我的流放生涯中的同伴和弟兄们,我们不是已经习惯了这种生活,觉得它比虚饰的浮华有趣得多吗?这些树林不比猜忌的朝廷更为安全吗?我们在这儿所感觉到的,只是时序的改变,那是上帝加于亚当的惩罚①;那冬天的风张舞着冰雪的爪牙,发出暴声的呼啸,即使当它砭刺着我的身体,使我寒冷而哆嗦的时候,我也会微笑着说:"这不是谄媚啊,它们就像是忠臣一样,谆谆提醒我所处的地位。"逆运也有它的好处,就像丑陋而有毒的蟾蜍,它的头上却顶着一颗珍贵的宝石。我们的这种生活,虽然与世间相遗弃,却可以听树木的谈话,溪中的流水便是大好的文章,一石之微,也暗寓着教训。每一件事物中间,都可以找到些益处来。我不愿改变这种生活。

阿米恩斯　殿下真是幸福,能把命运的顽逆说成了这样恬静而可爱的样子。

公爵　来,我们打鹿去吧。可是我心里却有些不忍,这种可怜的花斑的蠢物,本来是这荒凉的城市中的居民,在它们自己的领域之内,他们的肥圆的腰肉上却要受到箭镞的刺伤。

臣甲　不错,那忧愁的杰奎斯很为那事伤心,发誓说您在这上面比起您那篡位的兄弟是一个更大的篡位者。今天

---

①　亚当(Adam,人类的始祖)未逐出乐园之前,四季常春。

阿米恩斯大人跟我两人悄悄地躲在背后,瞧他躺在一株橡树底下。沿着林旁潺潺流去的溪水上面露出一根古老树根,有一只可怜的失群的牡鹿中了猎人的箭,奔到那边去喘气。真的,殿下,这头不幸的畜生发出了那样的呻吟,真要把它的皮囊都胀破了,一颗颗粗圆的泪珠怪可怜地争先恐后流到它无辜的鼻子上;忧愁的杰奎斯瞧着这头可怜的毛畜这样站在急流的小溪边,把眼泪添注在溪水里。

公爵 但是杰奎斯怎样说呢?他见了此情此景,不又要讲起一番道理来了吗?

臣甲 啊,是的,他做了一千种譬喻。起初他看见那鹿把眼泪浪费地流入了水流之中,便说:"可怜的鹿,你就像世人立遗嘱一样,把你所有的一切给了那已经有得太多的人。"于是,看它孤身独自,被它那些皮毛柔滑的朋友们所遗弃,便说:"不错,人倒了霉,朋友也不会来睬你了。"不久又有一群吃得饱饱的、无忧无虑的鹿跳过它的身边,也不停下来向它打个招呼。"嗯,"杰奎斯说,"奔过去吧,你们这批肥胖而富于脂肪的市民们;世事无非如此,那个可怜的破产的家伙,瞧他做什么呢?"他这样用最恶毒的话来辱骂着乡村、城市和宫廷的一切,甚至于骂着我们的这种生活;发誓说我们只是些篡位者、暴君或者比这更坏的人物,到这些畜生们的天然的居处来惊扰它们、杀害它们。

公爵　你们就在他做这种思索的时候离开了他吗?

臣甲　是的,殿下,就在他为了这头啜泣的鹿而流泪发议论的时候。

公爵　带我到那地方去,我喜欢趁他发愁的时候去见他,因为那时他最富于见识。

臣甲　我就领您去见他。(同下)

第二场
宫中一室

【弗莱德里克公爵、众臣及侍从上。

弗莱德里克 难道没有一个人看见她们吗？绝不会的；在我的宫廷里一定有奸人知情串通。

臣甲 我不曾听见谁说曾经看见她。她寝室里的侍女们都看她上了床，可是一早就看见床上没有她们的郡主了。

臣乙 殿下，那个常常逗您发笑的下贱小丑也失踪了。郡主的侍女希丝比利娅供认她曾经偷听到郡主跟她的姊姊常常称赞最近在摔跤赛中打败了强有力的查尔斯的那个汉子的技艺和人品。她说她相信不论她们到哪里去，那个少年一定是跟她们在一起的。

弗莱德里克 差人到他哥哥家里去，把那家伙抓来。要是他不在，就带他的哥哥来见我，我要叫他的哥哥去找他。马上去，这两个逃走的傻子一定要用心搜寻探访，非把她们寻回来不可。（众下）

第三场
奥列佛家门前

【奥兰多及亚当自相对方向上。

奥兰多　那边是谁?

亚当　啊!我的少爷吗?啊,我的善良的少爷!我的好少爷!啊,您叫人想起了老罗兰爵爷!唉,您为什么到这里来呢?您为什么这样好呢?为什么人家要爱您呢?为什么您是这样仁善、这样健壮、这样勇敢呢?为什么您这么傻,要去把那乖僻的公爵手下那个壮大的拳师打败呢?您的声誉是来得太快了。您不知道吗,少爷,有些人常会因为他们太好了,反而害了自己?您也正是这样。您的好处,好少爷,就是陷害您自身的圣洁的叛徒,唉,这算是一个什么世界,怀德的人会因为他们的德行而反遭毒手!

奥兰多 啊,怎么一回事?

亚当 唉,不幸的青年!不要走进这扇门来;在这屋子里潜伏着您一切美德的敌人呢。您的哥哥——不,不是哥哥,然而却是您父亲的儿子——不,他也不能称为他的儿子——他听见了人家称赞您的话,预备在今夜放火烧去您所住的屋子。要是这计划不成功,他还会想出别的法子来除掉您。他的阴谋给我偷听到了。这儿不是安身之处,这屋子不过是一所屠场,您要回避,您要警戒,别走进去。

奥兰多 什么,亚当,你要我到哪儿去?

亚当 随您到哪儿去都好,只要不在这儿。

奥兰多 什么,你要我去做个要饭的吗,还是在大路上做一个吃喝无耻的强盗?我只好走这种路,否则我就不知道怎么办。可是即使我有这种本事,我也不愿这样干,我宁愿忍受一个不念手足之情的凶狠的哥哥的恶意。

亚当 可是不要这样。我在您父亲手下侍候了这许多年,曾经辛辛苦苦把工钱省下了五百块。我把那笔钱存下,本来是预备等我没有气力做不动事的时候做养老之本,人一老不中用了,是会给人踢到角落里的。您拿了去吧。上帝给食物与乌鸦,他也不会忘记把麻雀喂饱,我这一把年纪,就悉听他的慈悲吧!钱就在这儿,我把它全都给了您了。让我做您的仆人。我虽然瞧上去这么老,可是我的气力还不错,因为我在年轻时候从不曾灌下过一滴猛烈的酒,也不曾鲁莽地贪欲伤身,所以我的老年是个生气勃勃的冬天,虽然结着严霜,却并不惨淡。让我跟着您去,我可以像一个年轻人一样,为您照料一切。

奥兰多 啊,好老人家!在你身上多么明白地表现出来古时那种忠心的服务,不是为着报酬,只是为了尽职而流着血汗!你是太不合时了。现在的人们努力工作,只是为着希望高升,等到目的一达到,便耽于安逸;你却不是这样。但是,可怜的老人家,你虽然这样辛辛苦苦地费尽培植的功夫,给你培植的却是一株不成材的树木,开不出一朵花来酬答你的殷勤。可是赶路吧,我们要在一块儿走。在我们没有把你年轻时的积蓄花完之前,一定要找到一处小小的安身的地方。

亚当 少爷,走吧。我愿意忠心地跟着您,直至喘尽最后一口气。从十七岁起我到这儿来,到现在快八十了,却要离开我的老地方。许多人在十七岁的时候都去追求幸运,但八十岁的人是不济的了;可是我只要能够有个好死,对得住我的主人,那么命运对我也不算无恩。(同下)

第四场
亚登森林

【罗瑟琳男装,西莉娅做牧羊女装束及试金石上。

罗瑟琳 天哪!我的精神多么疲乏啊。

试金石 我可不管我的精神,假如我的两腿不疲乏。

罗瑟琳 我简直想丢了我这身男装的脸,而像一个女人一样哭起来,可是我必须安慰安慰这位小娘子,穿褐衫短裤的,总该向穿裙子的显出一点勇气来才是。好,提起精神来吧,好爱莲娜。

西莉娅　请你担待担待我吧。我再也走不动了。

罗瑟琳　好,这儿就是亚登森林了。

试金石　唉,现在我到了亚登了。我真是个大傻瓜!在家里舒服得多哩。可是旅行人只好知足一点。

罗瑟琳　对了,好试金石。你们瞧,谁来了,一个年轻人和一个老头子在一本正经地讲话。

【柯林及西尔维斯上。

柯林　你那样不过叫她永远把你笑骂而已。

西尔维斯　啊,柯林,你要是知道我是多么爱她!

柯林　我有点猜得出来,因为我也曾经恋爱过呢。

西尔维斯　不,柯林,你现在老了,也就不能猜想了。虽然在你年轻的时候,你也像那些半夜二更在枕上翻来覆去的情人们一样真心。可是假如你的爱也是跟我差不多的——我想一定没有人有我那样的爱法——那么你为了你的痴心梦想,一定做出过不知多少可笑的事情来呢!

柯林　我做过一千种的傻事,现在都已忘记了。

西尔维斯　噢!那么你就是不曾诚心爱过。假如你记不得你为了爱情而做出来的一件最琐细的傻事,你就不算真的恋爱过。假如你不曾像我现在这样坐着絮絮讲你的姑娘的好处,使听的人不耐烦,你就不算真的恋爱过。假如你不曾突然离开你的同伴,像我的热情现在驱使着我一样,你也不算真的恋爱过。啊,菲苾!菲

芯!菲芯!(下)

罗瑟琳 唉,可怜的牧人!我在诊探你的痛处的时候,却不幸地找到我自己的创伤了。

试金石 我也是这样。我记得我在恋爱的时候,曾经把一柄剑在石头上摔碎,叫那趁夜里来和琴·史美尔幽会的那个家伙留心着我;我记得我曾经吻过她的洗衣棍子,也吻过被她那双皱裂的玉手挤过的母牛乳头;我记得我曾经把一颗豌豆荚权当作她而向她求婚,我剥出了两颗豆子,又把它们放进去,边流泪边说:"为了我的缘故,请您留着作个纪念吧。"我们这种多情种子都会做出一些古怪事儿来,但是我们既然都是凡人,一着了情魔是免不得要大发其痴劲的。

罗瑟琳 你的话聪明得出于你自己意料之外。

试金石 噢,我总不知道自己的聪明,除非有一天我给它绊跌断了我的腿骨。

罗瑟琳 天神,天神!这个牧人的痴心,很有几分像我自己的情形。

试金石 也有点像我的情形。可是在我似乎有点儿陈腐了。

西莉娅 请你们随便哪一位去问问那边的人,肯不肯让我们用金子向他买一点吃的东西。我简直要乏力死了。

试金石 喂,你这蠢货!

罗瑟琳 别响,傻子。他并不是你的一家人。

柯林　谁叫？

试金石　比你好一点的人,朋友。

柯林　要是他们不比我好一点,那可寒酸得太不像话啦。

罗瑟琳　对你说,别响。——您晚安,朋友。

柯林　晚安,好先生;各位晚安。

罗瑟琳　牧人,假如人情或是金银可以在这种荒野里换到一点款待的话,请你带我们到一处可以休息一下吃些东西的地方去好不好？这一位小姑娘赶路疲乏,快要晕过去了。

柯林　好先生,我可怜她,不是为我自己打算,只是为了她的缘故,但愿我有能力帮助她。可是我只是给别人看羊的,羊儿虽然归我饲养,羊毛却不归我剪。我的东家很小气,从不会修修福做点儿好事,而且他的草屋、他的羊群、他的牧场,现在都要出卖了。现在我们的牧舍里因为他不在家,没有一点可以给你们吃的东西,但是别管它有些什么,请你们来瞧瞧看,我对你们是极其欢迎的。

罗瑟琳　他的羊群和牧场预备卖给谁呢？

柯林　就是刚才你们看见的那个年轻汉子,他是从来不想要买什么东西的。

罗瑟琳　要是没有什么不对的地方,我请你把那草屋牧场和羊群都买下了,我们给你出钱。

西莉娅　我们还要加你的工钱。我欢喜这地方,很愿意在这儿消度我的时光。

柯林　这注家私一定可以成交。跟我来。要是你们打听过后,对于这块地皮、这种收益和这样的生活觉得中意的话,我愿意做你们十分忠心的仆人,马上用你们的钱去把它买来。(同下)

第五场
林中的另一部分

【阿米恩斯、杰奎斯及余人等上。

阿米恩斯　(唱)

　　　绿树高张翠幕,
　　　谁来偕我偃卧,
　　　翻将欢乐心声,
　　　学唱枝头鸟鸣:
　　盍来此?盍来此?盍来此?
　　　目之所接,
　　　　精神契一,
　　唯忧雨雪之将至。

杰奎斯　再来一个,再来一个,请你再唱下去。

阿米恩斯　那会叫您发起愁来的,杰奎斯先生。

杰奎斯　再好没有。请你再唱下去!我可以从一曲歌中抽出愁绪来,就像黄鼠狼吮啜鸡蛋一样。请你再唱下去吧!

阿米恩斯 我的喉咙很粗,我知道一定不能讨您的欢喜。

杰奎斯 我不要你讨我的欢喜;我只要你唱。来,再唱一阕。你是不是把它们叫作一阕一阕的?

阿米恩斯 随您高兴怎样叫吧,杰奎斯先生。

杰奎斯 不,我倒不去管它们叫什么名字,它们又不借我的钱。你唱起来吧!

阿米恩斯 既蒙敦促,我就勉为其难了。

杰奎斯 那么好,要是我会感谢什么人的,我一定会感谢你,可是人家所说的恭维就像是两只狗猿碰了头。倘使有人诚心感谢我,我就觉得好像我给了他一个铜子,所以他像一个叫花子似的向我道谢。来,唱起来吧,你们不唱的都不要作声。

阿米恩斯 好,我就唱完这支歌。列位,铺起食桌来吧;公爵就要到这株树下来喝酒了。他已经找了您整整一天啦。

杰奎斯 我已经躲避了他整整一天啦。他太喜欢辩论了,我不高兴跟他在一起。我想到的事情像他一样多,可是谢谢天,我的嘴却不像他那样会说。来,唱吧。

阿米恩斯 (唱,众和)

孰能敝屣尊荣,
来沐丽日光风,

　　　　觅食自求果腹，
　　　　一饱欣然意足；
　　盍来此？盍来此？盍来此？
　　　　目之所接，
　　　　精神契一，
　　　　唯忧雨雪之将至。

杰奎斯　昨天我曾经按着这调子作了一节，倒要献丑献丑。
阿米恩斯　我可以把它唱出来。
杰奎斯　是这样的：

　　　　倘有痴愚之徒，
　　　　忽然变成蠢驴，
　　　　趁着心性癫狂，
　　　　撇却财富安康，
　　特达米，特达米，特达米，
　　　　何为来此？
　　　　举目一视，
　　　　唯见傻瓜之遍地。

阿米恩斯　"特达米"是什么意思？
杰奎斯　这是希腊文里召唤傻子们排起圆圈来的一种咒语。——假如睡得成觉的话，我要睡觉去；假如睡不成,我就要把埃及地方一切头胎生的痛骂一顿①。

阿米恩斯 我可要找公爵去;他的点心已经预备好了。(各下)

第六场
林中的另一部分

【奥兰多及亚当上。

亚当 好少爷,我再也走不动了。唉!我要饿死了。让我在这儿躺下挺尸吧。再会了,好心的少爷!

奥兰多 啊,怎么啦,亚当!你再没有勇气了吗?再活一些时候,提起一点精神来,高兴点儿。要是这座古怪的林中有什么野东西,那么我倘不是给它吃了,一定会把它杀了来给你吃的。你并不是真就要死了,不过是在胡思乱想而已。为了我的缘故,提起精神来吧。把死神拖一拖住,我去一去就回来看你,要是我找不到什么可以给你吃的东西,我一定答应你死去;可是假如你在我没有回来之前便死去,那你就是看不起我的辛苦了。说得好!你瞧上去很高兴。我立刻就来。可是你躺在

---

① 《旧约·出埃及记》载上帝降罚埃及,凡埃及一切头胎生的皆遭瘟死;此处杰奎斯暗讽长公爵。

寒风里呢,来,我把你背到有遮阴的地方去。只要这块荒地里有活东西,你一定不会因为没有饭吃而饿死。振作起来吧,好亚当。(同下)

第七场
林中的另一部分

【食桌铺就。老公爵、阿米恩斯及流亡诸臣上。

公爵 我想他一定已经变成一头畜生了,因为我到处找不到他的人影。

臣甲 殿下,他刚刚走开去。方才他还在这儿很高兴地听人家唱歌。

公爵 要是浑身都不和谐的他,居然也会变得爱好起音乐来,那么天体上不久就要大起骚乱了。去找他来,对他说我要跟他谈谈。

臣甲 他自己来了,省了我一番跋涉。

【杰奎斯上。

公爵 啊,怎么啦,先生!这算什么,您的可怜的朋友们一定要千求万唤才把您请来吗?啊,您的神气很高兴哩!

杰奎斯 一个傻子,一个傻子!我在林中遇见一个傻子,一个身穿彩衣的傻子。唉,苦恼的世界!我确实遇见了一个傻子,正如我是靠着食物而活命的;他躺着晒太阳,用头头是道的话辱骂着命运女神,然而他仍然不过是个身穿彩衣的傻子。"早安,傻子,"我说。"不,先生,"他说,"等到老天保佑我发了财,您再叫我傻子吧。"①于是他从袋里掏出一只表来,用没有光彩的眼睛瞧着它,很聪明地说,"现在是十点钟了,我们可以从这里看出世界是怎样在变迁着:一小时之前还不过是九点钟,而再过一小时便是十一点钟了。照这样一小时一小时过去,我们越长越老,越老越不中用,这上面真是大有感慨可发。"我听了这个穿彩衣的傻子对着时间发挥了这一段玄理,我的胸头就像公鸡一样叫起来了,奇怪着傻子居然会有这样深刻的思想。我笑了个不停,在他的表上整整笑去了一个小时。啊,高贵的傻子! 可敬的傻子! 彩衣是最好的装束。

公爵 这是个怎么样的傻子?

杰奎斯 啊,可敬的傻子! 他曾经出入宫廷;他说凡是年轻貌美的小姐们,都是有自知之明的。他的头脑就像航海回来剩下的饼干那样干燥,其中的每一个角落却塞满了人生的经验,他都用杂乱的话儿随口说了出来。啊,我但愿我也是个傻子! 我想要穿一件花花的外套。

公爵 你可以有一件。

杰奎斯 这是我唯一要求的一身服装。只要你愿意把一切

---

① 成语有"愚人多福"(Fortune favours fools),故云。

以为我是个聪明人这种观念除掉,别让它蒙蔽了您的明鉴。同时要准许我有像风那样广大的自由,高兴吹着谁便吹着谁。傻子们是有这种权利的,那些最被我的傻话所挖苦的,最应该笑。殿下,为什么他们必须这样呢?这理由正和到教区礼拜堂去的路一样明白:被一个傻子用俏皮话讥刺了的,即使刺痛了,假如不装出一副若无其事的态度来,那么就显出聪明人的傻气,可以被傻子不经意一箭就刺穿,未免太傻了。给我穿一件彩衣,准许我说我心里的话。我一定会痛痛快快地把这染遍世界的丑恶的身体清洗个干净,假如他们肯耐心接受我的药方。

公爵 算了吧!我知道你会做出些什么来。

杰奎斯 我可以拿一根筹码打赌,我做的事会不好吗?

公爵 最坏不过的罪恶,就是指斥他人的罪恶。因为你自己也曾经是一个放纵兽欲的浪子。你要把你那身因你的胡闹而长起来的臃肿的脓疮、溃烂的恶病,向全世界播散。

杰奎斯 什么,呼斥人间的奢侈,难道便是对个人的攻击吗?人们的骄傲不是像海潮一样浩瀚地流着,直到它力竭而消退?假如我说城里的那些小户人家的妇女穿扮得像王公大人的女眷一样,我指明是哪一个女人了吗?谁能挺身出来说我说的是她,假如她的邻居也是和她一个样子?一个操着最微贱行业的人,假如心想我讥讽了他,说他的好衣服不是我出的钱,那不是恰恰把他的愚蠢合上了我说的话吗?照此看来,又有什么关系呢?给我看我的说话伤害了他什么地方:要是说得对,那是他自取其咎;假如他问心无愧,那么我的责骂就像是一头野鸭飞过,不干谁的事。——可是谁来了?

【奥兰多拔剑上。

奥兰多 停住,不准吃!

杰奎斯 嘿,我还不曾吃过呢。

奥兰多 而且也不会再给你吃,除非让饿肚子的人先吃过了。

杰奎斯 这头公鸡是哪儿来的?

公爵 朋友,你是因为落难而变得这样强横吗?还是因为生来就是瞧不起礼貌的粗汉子,一点儿不懂得规矩?

奥兰多 你第一下就猜中我了,困苦逼迫着我,使我不得不把温文的礼貌抛开一旁;可是我却是在都市生长,受过一点儿教养的。但是我吩咐你们停住。在我的事情没有办完之前,谁碰一碰这些果子,就得死。

杰奎斯 你要是不可理喻,那么我准得死。

公爵 你要什么?假如你不用暴力,客客气气地向我们说,我们一定会更客客气气地对待你的。

奥兰多 我快饿死了,给我吃。

公爵 请坐请坐,随意吃吧。

奥兰多 你说得这样客气吗?请你原谅我,我以为这儿的一切都是野蛮的,因此才装出这副暴横的威胁神气来。可是不论你们是些什么人,在这个人踪不到的荒野里,躺在凄凉的树荫下,不理会时间的消逝。假如你们曾经见过较好的日子,假如你们曾经到过鸣钟召集礼拜的地方,假如你们曾经参加过上流人的宴会,假如你们曾经揩过你们眼皮上的泪水,懂得怜悯和被怜悯的,那么让我的温文的态度格外感动你们:我抱着这样的希望,惭愧地藏好我的剑。

公爵 我们确曾见过好日子,曾经被神圣的钟声召集到教堂里去,参加过上流人的宴会,从我们的眼上揩去过被神圣的怜悯所感动而流下的眼泪。所以你不妨和和气气地坐下来,凡是我们可以帮忙满足你需要的地方,一定愿意效劳。

奥兰多 那么请你们暂时不要把东西吃掉,我就去像一只母鹿一样找寻我的小鹿,把食物喂给他吃。有一位可怜的老人家,全然出于好心,跟着我一瘸一拐地走了许多疲乏的路,两星期的劳瘁,他的高龄和饥饿累倒了他。除非等他饱餐了之后,我绝不接触一口食物。

公爵 快去找他,我们绝对不把东西吃掉,等着你回来。

奥兰多 谢谢!愿您好心有好报!(下)

公爵 你们可以看到不幸的不只是我们;这个广大的宇宙的舞台上,还有比我们所演出的更悲惨的场面呢。

杰奎斯 全世界是一个舞台,所有的男男女女不过是一些演员;他们都有下场的时候,也都有上场的时候。一个人的一生中扮演着好几个角色,他的表演可以分为七个时期。最初是婴孩,在保姆的怀中啼哭呕吐。然后是背着书包、满脸红光的学童,像蜗牛一样慢吞吞地拖着脚步,不情愿地呜咽着上学堂。然后是情人,像炉灶一样叹着气,写了一首悲哀的诗歌咏着他恋人的眉毛。然后是一个军人,满口发着古怪的誓,胡须长得像豹子一样,爱惜着名誉,动不动就要打架,在炮口上寻求着泡沫一样的荣名。然后是法官,胖胖圆圆的肚子塞满了阉鸡,凛然的眼光,整洁的胡须,满嘴都是格言和老生常谈;他这样扮了他的一个角色。第六个时期变成了精瘦的趿着拖鞋的龙钟老叟,鼻子上架着眼镜,腰边悬着钱袋;他那小心省下来的年轻时候的长袜子套在他皱瘪的小腿上宽大异常;他那朗朗的男子的口音又变成了孩子似的尖声,像是吹着风笛和哨子。终结着这段古怪的多事的历史的最后一场,是孩提时代的再现,全然的遗忘,没有牙齿,没有眼睛,没有口味,没有一切。

【奥兰多背亚当重上。

公爵　欢迎!放下你背上那位可敬的老人家,让他吃东西吧。

奥兰多　我代他向您竭诚道谢。

亚当　您真该代我道谢;我简直不能为自己向您开口道谢呢。

公爵 欢迎,请用吧。我还不会马上就来打扰你,问你的遭遇。给我们奏些音乐;贤卿,你唱吧。

阿米恩斯 (唱)

不惧冬风凛冽,

风威远难遽及

人世之寡情;

其为气也虽厉,

其牙尚非甚锐,

风体本无形。

噫嘻乎!且向冬青歌一曲:

友交皆虚妄,恩爱痴人逐。

噫嘻乎冬青!

可乐唯此生。

不愁冱天冰雪,

其寒尚难遽及,

受施而忘恩;

风皱满池碧水,

利刺尚难遽比,

捐旧之友人。

噫嘻乎!且向冬青歌一曲:

友交皆虚妄,恩爱痴人逐。

噫嘻乎冬青!

可乐唯此生。

公爵 照你刚才悄声儿老老实实告诉我的,你说你是好罗兰爵士的儿子,我看你的相貌也真的十分像他。如果不是假的,那么我真心欢迎你到这儿来。我便是敬爱你父亲的那个公爵。关于你其他的遭遇,到我的洞里来告诉我吧。好老人家,我们欢迎你像欢迎你的主人一样。搀扶着他。把你的手给我,让我明白你们一切的经过。(众下)

48　皆大欢喜

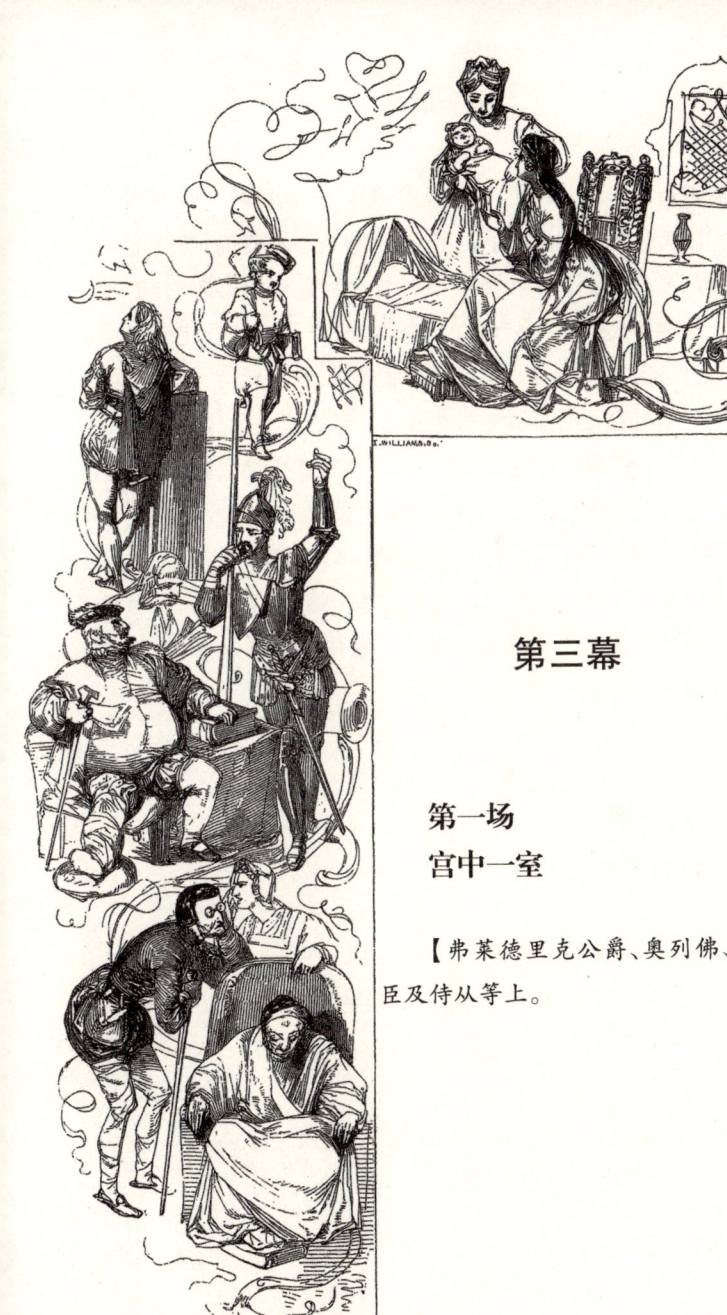

第三幕

第一场
宫中一室

【弗莱德里克公爵、奥列佛、众臣及侍从等上。

弗莱德里克 以后没有见过他!哼哼,不见得吧。倘不是因为仁慈在我的心里占了上风,有着你在眼前,我尽可以不必找一个不在的人出气的。可是你留心着吧,不论你的兄弟在什么地方,都得去给我找来。点起灯笼去寻访吧,在一年之内,要把他找到,不论死活,否则你不用再在我们的领土上过活了。你的土地和其他一切你自命为属于你的东西,值得没收的我们都要没收,除非你能够凭着你兄弟的招供洗刷去我们对你的怀疑。

奥列佛 求殿下明鉴!我从来就不曾喜欢过我的兄弟。

弗莱德里克 这可见你更是个坏人了。好,把他赶出去;吩咐官吏把他的房屋土地没收。赶快把这事办好,叫他滚蛋。(众下)

第二场
亚登森林

【奥兰多携纸上。

奥兰多 悬在这里吧,我的诗,证明我的爱情;
　　　　　你三重王冠的夜间的女王,请临视①,

---

① 三重王冠的女王指黛安娜(Diana)女神,因为她在天上为Luna,在地上为Diana,在幽冥为Proserpina。

从苍白的昊天,用你那贞洁的眼睛,
　　那支配我生命的,你那猎伴的名字①。
啊,罗瑟琳!这些树林将是我的书册,
　　我要在一片片树皮上镂刻下相思,
好让每一个来到此间的林中游客,
　　任何处见得到颂赞她美德的言辞。
走,走,奥兰多;去在每株树上刻着伊,
　　那美好的、幽娴的、无可比拟的人儿。(下)

---

　　① 狄安娜又为司狩猎的女神,又为处女的保护神,故奥兰多以罗瑟琳为她的猎伴。

【柯林及试金石上。

柯林 您喜欢不喜欢这种牧人的生活,试金石先生?

试金石 说老实话,牧人,按着这种生活本身说起来,倒是一种很好的生活;可是按着这是一种牧人的生活说起来,那就毫不足取了。照它的清静而论,我很喜欢这种生活;可是照它的寂寞而论,实在是一种很坏的生活。看到这种生活是在田间,很使我满意;可是看到它不是在宫廷里,那简直很无聊。你瞧,这是一种很经济的生活,因此倒怪合我的脾胃;可是它未免太寒碜了,因此我过不来。你懂不懂得一点哲学,牧人?

柯林 我只知道这一点儿:一个人越是害病,他越是不舒服;钱财、资本和知足,是人们缺少不来的三位好朋友;雨淋湿衣,火旺烧柴;好牧场产肥羊,天黑是因为没有了太阳;生来愚笨怪祖父,学而不慧师之惰。

试金石 这样一个人是天生的哲学家了。有没有到过宫廷里,牧人?

柯林 没有,不瞒您说。

试金石 那么你这人就该死了。

柯林 我希望不至于吧?

试金石 真的,你这人该死,就像一个煎得不好一面焦的鸡蛋。

柯林 因为没有到过宫廷里吗?请说说您的理由。

试金石 喏,要是你从来没有到过宫廷里,你就不曾见过好礼貌;要是你从来没有见过好礼貌,你的举止一定很坏;坏人就是有罪的人,有罪的人就该死。你的情形很危险呢,牧人。

柯林 一点不,试金石。在宫廷里算作好礼貌的,在乡野里就会变成可笑,正像乡下人的行为一到了宫廷里就显得寒碜一样。您对我说过你们在宫廷里只要见人打招呼就要吻手;要是宫廷里的老爷们都是牧人,那么这种礼貌就要嫌太腥臊了。

试金石 有什么证据?简单地说。来,说出理由来。

柯林 喏,我们的手常常要去碰着母羊。它们的毛,您知道,是很油腻的。

试金石 嘿,廷臣们的手上不是也要出汗的吗?羊身上的脂肪比起人身上的汗腻来,不是一样干净的吗?浅薄!浅薄!说出一个好一点的理由来,说吧。

柯林 而且,我们的手很粗糙。

试金石 那么你们的嘴唇格外容易感到它们。还是浅薄!再说一个充分一点的理由,说吧。

柯林 我们的手在给羊们包扎伤处的时候总是涂满了焦油,您要我们跟焦油接吻吗?宫廷里的老爷们手上都是涂着麝香的。

试金石 浅薄不堪的家伙!把你跟一块好肉比起来,你简直是一块给蛆虫吃的臭肉!用心听聪明人的教训吧:麝香是一只猫身上流出来的腥臊东西,它的来源比焦油脏得多呢。把你的理由修正修正吧,牧人。

柯林 您太会讲话了,我说不过您;我不说了。

试金石 你就甘心该死吗?上帝保佑你,浅薄的人!上帝把你好好针砭一下!你太不懂世事了。

柯林 先生,我是一个道地的做活人。我用自己的力量换饭吃换衣服穿;不跟别人结怨,也不妒羡别人的福气;瞧着人家得意我也高兴,自己倒了霉就自宽自解;我的最大的骄傲就是瞧我的母羊吃草、我的羔羊啜奶。

试金石 这又是你的一桩因为傻气而造下的孽:你把母羊和公羊拉拢在一起,靠着它们的配对来维持你的生活;给挂铃的羊当龟奴,替一头歪脖子的老王八公羊把才一岁的雌儿骗诱失身,也不想到合配不合配。要是你不会因此而下地狱,那么也没有人给魔鬼牧羊了。我想不出你有什么被豁免的希望。

柯林 盖尼米德大官人来了,他是我的新主妇的哥哥。

【罗瑟琳读一张字纸上。

罗瑟琳 从东印度到西印度找遍奇珍,
没有一颗珠玉比得上罗瑟琳。
她的名声随着好风播满诸城,
整个世界都在仰慕着罗瑟琳。
画工描摹下一幅幅倩影真真,
都要黯然无色一见了罗瑟琳。
任何的样貌都不用铭记在心,

单单牢记住了美丽的罗瑟琳。

试金石　我可以给您这样凑韵下去凑他整整的八年,吃饭和睡觉的时间除外。这好像是一连串上市去卖奶油的好大娘。

罗瑟琳　啐,傻子!

试金石　试一下看:

要是公鹿找不到母鹿很伤心,
不妨叫它前去寻找那罗瑟琳。
倘说是没有一只猫儿不叫春,
心同此情有谁能责怪罗瑟琳?
冬天的衣裳棉花应该衬得温,
免得冻坏了娇怯怯的罗瑟琳。
割下的田禾必须捆得端端整,
一车的禾捆上装着个罗瑟琳。
最甜蜜的果子皮儿酸痛了唇,
这种果子的名字便是罗瑟琳。
有谁想找到玫瑰花开香喷喷,
就会找到爱的棘刺和罗瑟琳。

这简直是胡扯的歪诗。您怎么也会给这种东西沾上了呢?

罗瑟琳　别多嘴,你这蠢傻瓜!我在一株树上找到它们的。

试金石　真的,这株树生的果子太坏。

【西莉娅读一张字纸上。

罗瑟琳 静些!我的妹妹读着些什么来了;站旁边去。
西莉娅 为什么这里是一片荒碛?

　　因为没有人居住吗? 不然,
我要叫每株树长起喉舌,

　　吐露出温文典雅的语言:
或是慨叹着生命一何短,

　　匆匆跑完了游子的行程,
只需把手掌轻轻翻个转,

　　便早已终结人们的一生;
或是感怀着旧盟今已冷,

　　同心的契友忘却了故交;
但我要把最好树枝选定,

　　缀附在每行诗句的终梢,
罗瑟琳三个字小名美妙,

　　向普世的读者遍告周知。
莫看她苗条的一身娇小,

　　宇宙间的精华尽萃于兹;
造物当时曾向自然诏示,

　　吩咐把所有的绝世姿才,
向纤纤一躯中合炉熔制,

　　累天工费去不少的安排:

负心的海伦醉人的脸蛋①,

 克莉奥佩特拉威仪丰容②。

阿塔兰忒的柳腰儿款摆③,

 鲁克丽西娅的节操贞松④:

劳动起玉殿上诸天仙众,

 造成这十全十美罗瑟琳;

荟萃了各式的妍媚万种,

 选出一副俊脸目秀精神。

上天给她这般恩赐优渥,

 我命该终生做她的臣仆。

罗瑟琳 啊,最温柔的宣教师!您的恋爱的说教是多么啰唆,叫您的教民听了厌烦,可是您却也不喊一声:"请耐心一点,好人们。"

西莉娅 啊!朋友们,退后去!牧人,稍为走开一点;跟他去,小子。

试金石 来,牧人,让我们堂堂退却:大小箱笼都不带,只带

---

 ① 海伦,即 Heien of Troy,因不贞于其夫米尼劳斯(Menelaus),故云"负心"。

 ② 克利奥佩特拉(Cleopatra),埃及女王,参看莎翁悲剧《女王殉国记》。

 ③ 阿塔兰忒(Atalanta),希腊传说中善疾走的美女。

 ④ 鲁克丽西娅(Lucretia),莎翁叙事诗 *The Rape of Lucrece* 中的主角。

一个头陀袋。(柯林、试金石下)

西莉娅 你有没有听见这种诗句?

罗瑟琳 啊,是的,我都听见了。

西莉娅 但是你听见你的名字被人家悬挂起来,还刻在这种树上,不觉得奇怪吗?

罗瑟琳 人家说一件奇事过了九天便不足为奇。在你没有来之前,我已经过了第七天了。瞧,这是我在一株棕榈树上找到的。自从毕达哥拉斯的时候以来,我从不曾被人这样用诗句咒过;那时我是一只爱尔兰的老鼠,现在简直记也记不起来了①。

西莉娅 你想这是谁干的?

罗瑟琳 是个男人吗?

西莉娅 而且有一根链条,是你从前带过的,套在他的颈上。你脸红了吗?

罗瑟琳 请你告诉我是谁?

西莉娅 主啊!主啊!朋友们见面真不容易;可是两座高山也许会给地震搬了家而碰起头来。

罗瑟琳 哎,但是究竟是谁呀?

西莉娅 真的猜不出来吗?

罗瑟琳 哎,我使劲地央求你告诉我他是谁。

---

① 毕达哥拉斯(Pythagoras),为主张灵魂轮回说的古希腊哲学家。念咒驱除老鼠为爱尔兰人的一种迷信习俗。

西莉娅　奇怪啊！奇怪啊！奇怪到无可再奇怪的奇怪！奇怪而又奇怪！说不出来的奇怪！

罗瑟琳　我要脸红起来了！你以为我打扮得像个男人，就会在精神上也穿起男装来了吗？你再耽延一刻不再说出来，就要累我在汪洋大海里做茫茫的探索了。请你快快告诉我他是谁，不要吞吞吐吐。我倒希望你是个口吃的，那么你也许会把这个保守着秘密的名字不期然地打你嘴里吐了出来，就像酒从窄口的瓶里倒出来一样，不是一点都倒不出，就是一下子出来了许多。求求你拔去你嘴里的塞子，让我饮着你的消息吧。

西莉娅　那么你要把那人儿一口气吞下肚里去是不是？

罗瑟琳　他是上帝造下来的吗？是个什么样子的人？他的头戴上一顶帽子显不显得寒碜？他的下巴留着一把胡须像不像个样儿？

西莉娅　不，他只有一点点儿胡须。

罗瑟琳　哦，要是这家伙知道好歹，上帝会再给他一些的。要是你立刻就告诉我他的下巴是怎么一个样子，我愿意等候他长起须来。

西莉娅　他就是年轻的奥兰多，一下子把那拳师的脚跟和你的心一起绊跌了个筋斗的。

罗瑟琳　哎，取笑人的让魔鬼抓了去；像一个老老实实的好姑娘似的，规规矩矩说吧。

西莉娅　真的，姊姊，是他。

罗瑟琳　奥兰多?

西莉娅　奥兰多。

罗瑟琳　哎哟!我这一身大衫短裤该怎么办呢?你看见他的时候他在做些什么?他说些什么?他瞧上去怎样?他穿着些什么?他为什么到这儿来?他问起我吗?他住在哪儿?他怎样跟你分别的?你什么时候再去看他?用一个字回答我。

西莉娅　你一定先要给我向卡冈都亚①借一张嘴来才行,像我们这时代的人,一张嘴里是装不下这么大的一个字的。要是一句句都用"是"和"不"回答起来,也比考问教理还麻烦呢。

罗瑟琳　可是他知道我在这林子里,打扮作男人的样子吗?他是不是跟摔跤的那天一样有精神?

西莉娅　回答情人的问题,就像数微尘的粒数一般为难。你好好听我讲我怎样找到他的,静静地体味着吧。我看见他在一株树底下,像一颗落下来的橡果。

罗瑟琳　树上会落下这样的果子来,那真可以说是神树了。

西莉娅　好小姐,听我说。

罗瑟琳　讲下去。

西莉娅　他直挺挺地躺在那儿,像一个受伤的武士。

---

① 卡冈都亚(Gargantua),法国诙谐文学家拉伯雷(Rabelais)著作中的饕餮巨人,能一口吞下五个香客。

罗瑟琳 虽然这种样子有点可怜,可是地上躺着这样一个人,倒也是很合适的。

西莉娅 喊你的舌头停步吧;它简直随处乱跳。——他打扮得像个猎人。

罗瑟琳 哎哟,糟了!他要来猎取我的心了。

西莉娅 我唱歌的时候不要别人和着唱;你缠得我弄错拍子了。

罗瑟琳 你不知道我是个女人吗?我心里想到什么,便要说出来。好人儿,说下去吧。

西莉娅 你已经打断了我的话头。且慢!他不是来了吗?

罗瑟琳 是他;我们躲在一旁瞧着他吧。

【奥兰多及杰奎斯上。

杰奎斯 多谢相陪!可是说老实话,我倒是喜欢一个人清静些。

奥兰多 我也是这样。可是为了礼貌的关系,我多谢您的做伴。

杰奎斯 上帝和您同在!让我们越少见面越好。

奥兰多 我希望我们还是不要相识的好。

杰奎斯 请您别再在树皮上写情诗糟蹋树木了。

奥兰多 请您别再用难听的声调念我的诗,把它们糟蹋了。

杰奎斯 您的情人的名字是罗瑟琳吗?

奥兰多 正是。

杰奎斯 我不喜欢她的名字。

奥兰多 她取名的时候,并没有打算要您喜欢。

杰奎斯 她的身材怎样?

奥兰多 恰恰够得到我的心头那样高。

杰奎斯 您怪会说俏皮的回答。您是不是跟金匠们的妻子有点儿交情,因此把戒指上的警句都默记了下来?

奥兰多 不,我都是用彩画的挂帏上的话儿来回答您,您的问题也是从那儿学来的。

杰奎斯 您的口才很敏捷,我想是用阿塔兰忒的脚跟做成的。我们一块儿坐下来好不好?我们两人要把世界痛骂一顿,大发一下牢骚。

奥兰多 我不愿责骂世上的有生之灵,除了我自己;因为我知道自己的错处最明白。

杰奎斯 您的最坏的错处就是要恋爱。

奥兰多 我不愿用这个错处来换取您的最好的美德。您真叫我腻烦。

杰奎斯 说老实话,我遇见您的时候,本来是在找一个傻子。

奥兰多 他掉在溪水里淹死了,您向水里一望,就可以瞧见他。

杰奎斯 我只瞧见我自己的影子。

奥兰多 那我以为倘不是个傻子,定然是个废物。

杰奎斯 我不想再跟您在一起了。再见,多情的公子。

奥兰多 我巴不得您走。再会,忧愁的先生。(杰奎斯下)

罗瑟琳 我要像一个无礼的小厮一样去跟他说话,跟他捣捣乱。——听见我的话吗,树林里的人?

奥兰多 很好,你有什么话说?

罗瑟琳 请问现在是几点钟?

奥兰多 你应该问我现在是什么时辰。树林里哪来的钟?

罗瑟琳 那么树林里也不会有真心的情人了,否则每分钟的叹气,每点钟的呻吟,该会像时钟一样计算出时间的懒懒的脚步来的。

奥兰多 为什么不说时间的快步呢?那样说不对吗?

罗瑟琳 不对,先生。时间对于各种人有各种的步法。我可以告诉你时间对于谁是走慢步的,对于谁是跨着细步走的,对于谁是奔着走的,对于谁是立定不动的。

奥兰多 请问时间对于谁是跨着细步走的?

罗瑟琳 呃,对于一个订了婚还没有成礼的姑娘,时间是跨着细步有气无力地走着的,即使这中间只有一星期,也似乎有七年那样难过。

奥兰多 对于谁时间是走着慢步的?

罗瑟琳 对于一个不懂拉丁文的牧师,或是一个不害痛风的富翁:一个因为不能读书而睡得很酣畅,一个因为没有痛苦而活得很高兴;一个可以不必辛辛苦苦地钻研,一个不知道有贫穷的艰困。对于这种人,时间是走着慢步的。

奥兰多 对于谁它是奔着走的?

罗瑟琳 对于一个上绞架的贼子,因为虽然他尽力放慢脚步,他还是觉得到得太快了。

奥兰多 对于谁它是静止不动的?

罗瑟琳 对于在休假中的律师,因为他们在前后开庭的时期之间,完全昏睡过去,不觉到时间的移动。

奥兰多 可爱的少年,你住在哪儿?

罗瑟琳 跟这位牧羊姑娘,我的妹妹,住在这儿的树林边。

奥兰多 你是本地人吗?

罗瑟琳 跟那只你看见的兔子一样,它的住处就是它生长的地方。

奥兰多 住在这种穷乡僻壤,你的谈吐却很高雅。

罗瑟琳 好多人都曾经这样说我。其实是因为我有一个修行的老伯父,他本来是在城市里生长的,是他教导我讲话;他曾经在宫廷里谈过恋爱,因此很懂得交际的门槛。我曾经听他发过许多反对恋爱的议论。多谢上帝我不是个女人,不会犯到他所归咎于一般女性的那许多心性轻浮的罪恶。

奥兰多 你记不记得他所说的女人的罪恶当中主要的几桩?

罗瑟琳 没有什么主要不主要的,跟两个铜子相比一样,全差不多;每一件过失似乎都十分严重,可是立刻又有一件出来可以赛过它。

奥兰多 请你说几件看看。

罗瑟琳 不,我的药是只给病人吃的。这座树林里常常有一个人来往,在我们的嫩树皮上刻满了"罗瑟琳"的名字,把树木糟蹋得不成样子;山楂树上挂起了诗篇,荆棘枝上吊悬着哀歌,说来说去都是把罗瑟琳的名字捧作神明。要是我碰见了那个卖弄风情的家伙,我一定要好好给他一番教训,因为他似乎害着相思病。

奥兰多 我就是那个给爱情折磨的他。请你告诉我你有什么医治的方法。

罗瑟琳 我伯父所说的那种记号在你身上全找不出来,他曾经告诉我怎样可以看出来一个人是在恋爱着。我可以断定你一定不是那个草扎的笼中的囚人。

奥兰多 什么是他所说的那种记号呢?

罗瑟琳 一张瘦瘦的脸庞,你没有;一双眼圈发黑的凹陷的眼睛,你没有;一副懒得跟人家交谈的神气,你没有;一脸忘记了修薙的胡子,你没有——可是那我可以原谅你,因为你的胡子本来就像小兄弟的产业一样少得可怜。而且你的袜子上应当是不套袜带的,你的帽子上应当是不结帽纽的,你的袖口的纽扣应当是脱开的,你的鞋子上的带子应当是松散的,你身上的每一处都要表示出一种不经心的疏懒。可是你却不是这样一个人;你把自己打扮得这么齐整,瞧你倒有点顾影自怜,全不像在爱着什么人。

奥兰多 美貌的少年,我希望我能使你相信我是在恋爱。

罗瑟琳 我相信!你还是叫你的爱人相信吧。我可以断定,她即使容易相信你,她嘴里也是不肯承认的,这也是女人们不老实的一点。可是说老实话,你真的便是把恭维着罗瑟琳的诗句悬挂在树上的那家伙吗?

奥兰多 少年,我凭着罗瑟琳的玉手向你起誓,我就是他,那个不幸的他。

罗瑟琳 可是你真的像你诗上所说的那样热恋着吗?

奥兰多 什么也不能表达我的爱情的深切。

罗瑟琳 爱情不过是一种疯狂。我对你说,人们对待有了爱情的人,是应该像对待一个疯子一样,把他关在黑屋子里用鞭子抽一顿的。那么为什么他们不用这种处罚的方法来医治爱情呢?因为那种疯病是极其平常的,就是拿鞭子的人也在恋爱哩。可是我有医治它的法子。

奥兰多 你曾经医治过什么人吗?

罗瑟琳 是的,医治过一个。法子是这样的:他假想我是他的爱人,他的情妇,我叫他每天都来向我求爱;那时我是一个善变的少年,便一会儿伤心,一会儿温存,一会儿翻脸,一会儿思慕,一会儿欢喜;骄傲、古怪、刁钻、浅薄、轻浮,有时满眼的泪,有时满脸的笑。什么情感都来一点儿,但没有一种是真切的,就像大多数的孩子们和女人们一样,有时喜欢他,有时讨厌他,有时讨好他,有时冷淡他,有时为他哭泣,有时把他唾弃。我这样把我这位求爱者从疯狂的爱逼到真的疯狂起来,以至于抛弃人世,做起隐士来了。我用这种方法治好了他,我也可以用这种方法把你的心肝洗得干干净净,像一颗没有毛病的羊心一样,再没有一点爱情的痕迹。

奥兰多 我不愿意治好,少年。

罗瑟琳 我可以把你治好,假如你把我叫作罗瑟琳,每天到我的草屋里来向我求爱。

奥兰多 凭着我的恋爱的真诚,我愿意。告诉我你住在什么地方。

罗瑟琳 跟我去,我可以指点给你看,一路上你也要告诉我你住在林中的什么地方。去吗?

奥兰多 很好,好孩子。

罗瑟琳 不,你一定要叫我罗瑟琳。来,妹妹,我们去吧。

(同下)

第三场
林中的另一部分

【试金石及奥德蕾上;杰奎斯随后。

试金石 快来,好奥德蕾,我去把你的山羊赶来。怎样,奥德蕾?我还不曾是你的好人儿吗?我这副粗鲁的神气你中意吗?

奥德蕾 您的神气!天老爷保佑我们!什么神气?

试金石 我陪着你和你的山羊在这里,就像那最会梦想的诗人奥维德在一群哥特人中间一样①。

杰奎斯 (旁白)唉,学问装在这么一副躯壳里,比乔武住在草棚里更坏②!

试金石 要是一个人写的诗不能叫人懂,他的才情不能叫人理解,那比之小客栈里开出一张大账单来还要命。真的,我希望神们把你变得诗意一点。

奥德蕾 我不懂得什么叫作"诗意一点"。那是一句好话,一件好事情吗?那是诚实的吗?

---

① 奥维德(Ovid),罗马诗人;歌斯人(the Goths),蹂躏罗马帝国的蛮族。

② 乔武化凡人至腓力基亚(Phrygia),居民咸拒之门外,惟Philemon 与 Baucis 二老夫妇留之宿其草舍中。

试金石　老实说,不,因为最真实的诗是最虚妄的。情人们都富于诗意,他们在诗里发的誓,可以说都是情人们的假话。

奥德蕾　那么您愿意老天爷把我变得诗意一点吗?

试金石　是的,不错。因为你发誓说你是贞洁的,假如你是个诗人,我就可以希望你说的是假话了。

奥德蕾　您不愿意我贞洁吗?

试金石　对了,除非你生得难看;因为贞洁跟美貌碰在一起,就像在糖里再加蜜。

杰奎斯　(旁白)好一个有见识的傻瓜!

奥德蕾　好,我生得不好看,因此我求求老天爷让我贞洁吧。

试金石　真的,把贞洁丢给一个丑陋的懒女人,就像把一块好肉盛在龌龊的盆子里。

奥德蕾　我不是个懒女人,虽然我谢谢老天爷我是丑陋的。

试金石　好吧,感谢老天爷把丑陋赏给了你!懒惰也许会跟着来的。可是不管这些,我一定要跟你结婚。为了这事我已经去见过邻村的牧师奥列佛·马坦克斯特师傅,他已经答应在这儿树林里会我,给我们配对。

杰奎斯　(旁白)我倒要瞧瞧这场热闹。

奥德蕾　好,老天爷保佑我们快活吧!

试金石　阿门!倘使是一个胆小的人,也许不敢贸然从事,因为这儿没有庙宇,只有树林,没有宾众,只有一些出角的畜生。但这有什么要紧呢？放出勇气来！角虽然讨厌,却也是少不来的①。人家说:"许多人有数不清的家私。"对了,许多人也有数不清的好角儿。好在那是他老婆陪嫁来的妆奁,不是他自己弄到手的。出角吗？有什么要紧？只有苦人儿才出角吗？不,不,最高贵的鹿和最寒碜的鹿长的角儿一样大呢。那么单身汉便算是好福气吗？不,城市总比乡村好些,已婚者隆起的额角,也要比未婚者平坦的额角体面得多;懂得几手击剑法的,总比一点不会的好些,因此有角也总比没角强。奥列佛师傅来啦。

【奥列佛·马坦克斯特师傅上。

试金石 奥列佛·马坦克斯特师傅,您来得巧极了。您是就在这树下替我们把事情办了呢,还是让我们跟您到您的教堂里去？

马坦克斯特 这儿没有人可以把这女人做主嫁出去吗？

试金石 我不要别人把她布施给我。

马坦克斯特 真的,她一定要有人做主许嫁,否则这种婚姻便不合法。

杰奎斯 （上前）进行下去,进行下去。我可以把她许嫁。

试金石 晚安,某某先生！您好,先生？欢迎欢迎！上次多蒙照顾,不胜感激。我很高兴看见您。我现在有一点

---

① "出角"即"当王八"。

点儿小事,先生。哎,请戴上帽子。

杰奎斯　你要结婚了吗,傻瓜?

试金石　先生,牛有轭,马有勒,猎鹰腿上挂金铃,人非木石岂无情?鸽子也要亲个嘴儿。女大当嫁,男大当婚。

杰奎斯　像你这样有教养的人,却愿意在一棵树底下像叫花子那样成亲吗?到教堂里去,找一位可以告诉你们婚姻的意义的好牧师。要是让这个家伙把你们像钉墙板似的钉在一起,你们中间总有一个人会像没有晒干的木板一样干缩起来,越变越弯的。

试金石　(旁白)我倒以为让他给我主婚比别人好一点,因为瞧他的样子是不会像样地主持婚礼的。假如结婚结得草率一些,以后我可以借口离弃我的妻子。

杰奎斯　你跟我来,让我指教指教你。

试金石　来,好奥德蕾。我们一定得结婚,否则我们只好通奸。再见,好奥列佛师傅,不是

　　亲爱的奥列佛!
　　勇敢的奥列佛!
　　请你不要把我丢弃;①

而是

　　走开去,奥列佛!
　　滚开去,奥列佛!

---

① "亲爱的奥列佛"三句为俗歌中的断句。

我们不要你行婚礼。(杰奎斯、试金石、奥德蕾同下)

马坦克斯特 不要紧,这一批荒唐的浑蛋谁也不能讥笑掉我的饭碗。(下)

第四场
林中的另一部分

【罗瑟琳及西莉娅上。

罗瑟琳 别跟我讲话;我要哭了。

西莉娅 你就哭吧。可是你还得想一想男人是不该流眼泪的。

罗瑟琳 但我岂不是有应该哭的理由吗?

西莉娅 理由是再充分不过的了,所以你哭吧。

罗瑟琳 瞧他的头发的颜色,就可以看出来他是个坏东西。

西莉娅 比犹大①的头发颜色略为深些,他的接吻就是犹大一脉相传下来的。

罗瑟琳 凭良心说一句,他的头发颜色很好。

西莉娅 那颜色好极了。栗色是最好的颜色。

罗瑟琳 他的接吻神圣得就像圣餐面包触到唇边一样。

西莉娅 他买来了一对狄安娜用过的嘴唇;一个凛若冰霜的尼姑也不会吻得像他那样虔诚;他的嘴唇里就有着冷冰冰的贞洁。

罗瑟琳 可是他为什么发誓说今天早上要来,却偏偏不来呢?

西莉娅 不用说,他这人没有半分真心。

罗瑟琳 你是这样想吗?

西莉娅 是的。我想他不是个扒手,也不是个盗马贼;可是要说起他的爱情真不真,那么我想他就像一只盖好了的空杯子,或是一枚蛀空了的硬壳果一样空心。

罗瑟琳 他的恋爱不是真心吗?

西莉娅 他在恋爱的时候,他是真心的;可是我以为他并不在恋爱。

---

① 犹大(Judas),出卖耶稣之门徒。

罗瑟琳　你不是听见他发誓说他的的确确在恋爱吗?

西莉娅　从前说是,现在却不一定是;而且情人们发的誓,是和堂倌嘴里的话一样靠不住的,他们都是惯报虚账的家伙。他在这儿树林子里跟公爵你的父亲在一块儿呢。

罗瑟琳　昨天我碰见公爵,跟他谈了好久。他问我的父母是怎样的人,我对他说,我的父母跟他一样高贵。他大笑着让我走了。可是我们现在有像奥兰多这么一个人,还要谈父亲做什么呢?

西莉娅　啊,好一个出色的人!他写得一手好诗,讲得一口漂亮话,发着动听的誓,再堂而皇之地毁了誓,同时碎了他情人的心;正如一个拙劣的枪手,骑在马上一面歪,像一头好鹅一样把他的枪杆折断了。但是年轻人凭着血气和痴劲做出来的事,总是很出色的。——谁来了?

【柯林上。

柯林　姑娘和大官人,你们不是常常问起那个害相思病的牧人,那天你们不是看见他和我坐在草地上,称赞着他的情人,那个盛气凌人的牧羊女吗?

西莉娅　嗯,他怎样啦?

柯林　要是你们想看一本认真扮演的好戏,一面是因为情痴而容颜惨白,一面是因为傲慢而满脸绯红。只要稍走几步路,我可以领你们去,看一个痛快。

罗瑟琳　啊！来,让我们去吧。在恋爱中的人,喜欢看人家相恋。带我们去看。我将要在他们的戏文里当一名重要的角色。(同下)

第五场
林中的另一部分

【西尔维斯及菲苾上。

西尔维斯　亲爱的菲苾,不要讥笑我,请不要,菲苾!您可以说您不爱我,但不要说得那样狠。习惯于杀人的硬心肠的刽子手,在把斧头向低俯的颈项上劈下的时候也要先说一声对不起。难道您会比这种靠着流血为生的人心肠更硬吗?

【罗瑟琳、西莉娅及柯林自后上。

菲苾　我不愿做你的刽子手。我逃避你,因为我不愿伤害你。你对我说我的眼睛会杀人,这种话当然说得很好听,很动人。眼睛本来是最柔弱的东西,一见了些微尘就会胆小得关起门来,居然也会给人叫作暴君、屠夫和凶手!现在我使劲地抡起白眼瞧着你,假如我的眼睛能够伤人,那么让它们把你杀死了吧:现在你可以假装晕过去了啊!嘿,现在你可以倒下去了呀,假如你并不倒下去,哼!羞啊,羞啊,你可别再胡说,说我的眼睛是凶手了。现在你且把我的眼睛加在你身上的伤痕拿出来看。单单用一枚针儿划了一下,也会有一点疤痕;握着一根灯芯草,你的手掌上也会有一刻儿留着痕迹。可是我的眼光现在向你投射,却不曾伤了你:我相信眼睛里是绝没有可以伤人的力量的。

西尔维斯 啊,亲爱的菲苾,要是有一天——也许那一天就近在眼前——您在谁清秀的脸庞上看出了爱情的力量,那时您就会感觉到爱情的利箭所加在您心上的无形的创伤了。

菲苾 可是在那一天没有到来之前,你不要走近我吧。如果有那一天,那么你可以用你的讥笑来凌虐我,却不用可怜我。因为不到那时候,我总不会可怜你的。

罗瑟琳 (上前)为什么呢,请问?谁是你的母亲,生下了你来,把这个不幸的人这般侮辱,如此欺凌?你生得不漂亮——老实说,我看你还是晚上不用点蜡烛就钻到被窝里去的好——难道就该这样骄傲而无情吗?——怎么,这是什么意思?你望着我做什么?我瞧你不过是一件天生的粗货罢了。他妈的!我想她要打算迷住我哩。不,老实说,骄傲的姑娘,你别做梦吧!凭着你的黑水一样的眉毛,你的乌丝一样的头发,你的黑玻璃球一样的眼睛,或是你的乳脂一样的脸庞,可不能叫我为你倾倒呀。——你这蠢牧人儿,干吗你要追随着她,像是挟着雾雨而来的南风?你是比她漂亮一千倍的男人。都是因为有了你们这种傻瓜,世上才有那许多难看的孩子。叫她得意的是你的恭维,不是她的镜子;听了你的话,她便觉得她自己比她本来的容貌美得多了。——可是,姑娘,你自己得放明白些。跪下来,斋戒谢天,赐给你这么好的一个爱人。我得向你耳边讲句体己的话,有买主的时候赶快卖去了吧,你不是到处都有销路的。求求这位大哥恕了你,爱他,接受他的好意。生得丑再要瞧不起人,那才是奇丑无比了。——好,牧人,你拿了她去。再见吧。

菲苾　可爱的青年,请您把我骂一整年吧。我宁愿听您的骂,不要听这人的恭维。

罗瑟林　他爱上了她的丑样子,她爱上了我的怒气。倘使真有这种事,那么她一扮起了怒容来答复你,我便会用刻薄的话儿去治她。——你为什么这样瞧着我?

菲苾　我对您没有怀着恶意呀。

罗瑟林　请你不要爱我吧,我这人是比醉后发的誓更靠不住的,而且我又不喜欢你。你要知道我家在何处,请到这儿附近的那簇橄榄树的地方来寻访好了。——我们去吧,妹妹。——牧人,着力追求她。——来,妹妹。——牧女,待他好一点儿,别那么骄傲;整个世界

上生眼睛的人,都不会像他那样把你当作天仙的。——来,瞧我们的羊群去。(罗瑟琳、西莉娅、柯林同下)

菲苾　过去的诗人,现在我明白了你的话果然是真:"谁个情人不是一见就钟情?"①

西尔维斯　亲爱的菲苾——

菲苾　啊!你怎么说,西尔维斯?

西尔维斯　亲爱的菲苾,可怜我吧!

菲苾　唉,我为你伤心呢,温柔的西尔维斯。

西尔维斯　同情之后,必有安慰;要是您见我为了爱情伤心而同情我,那么只要把您的爱给我,您就可以不用再同情,我也无须再伤心了。

菲苾　你已经得到我的爱了。咱们不是像邻居么要好着吗?

西尔维斯　我要的是您。

菲苾　啊,那就是贪心了。西尔维斯,从前我讨厌你,可是现在我也不是对你有什么爱情。不过你既然讲爱情讲得那么好,我本来是讨厌跟你在一起的,现在我可以忍受你了。我还有事儿要差遣你呢,可是除了你自己因为供我差遣而感到的欣喜以外,可不用希望我还会用

---

①　过去的诗人指马洛(Christopher Marlowe);"谁个情人不是一见就钟情?"一句系马洛所作叙事诗 *Hero and Leander* 中之语。

什么来答谢你。

西尔维斯 我的爱情是这样圣洁而完整,我又是这样不蒙眷顾,因此只要能够拾些人家收获过后留下来的残穗,我也以为是一次最丰富的收成了;随时略为给我一个不经意的微笑,我就可以靠着它而活命。

菲苾 你认识刚才对我讲话的那个少年吗?

西尔维斯 不大熟悉,但我常常遇见他,他已经把本来属于那个老头儿的草屋和地产都买下来了。

菲苾 不要以为我爱他,虽然我问起他。他只是个淘气的孩子,可是倒很会讲话。但是空话我理它作甚?然而说话的人要是能够讨听话的人欢喜,那么空话也是很好的。他是个标致的青年,不算顶标致。当然他是太骄傲了,然而他的骄傲很配他。他长得倒是一个漂亮的汉子,顶好的地方就是他的脸色;他的舌头刚刚得罪了人,用眼睛一瞟就补偿过来了。他的个儿不算高,然而照他的年纪说起来也就够高。他的腿不过如此,但也还好。他的嘴唇红得很美,比他那张白脸上掺和着的红色更烂熟更浓艳,一个是大红,一个是粉红。西尔维斯,有些女人假如也像我一样像他这么评头品足起来,一定会马上爱上他的;可是我呢,我不爱他,也不恨他,然而我有应该格外恨他的理由。凭什么他要骂我呢?他说我的眼珠黑,我的头发黑;现在我记起来了,他嘲笑着我呢。我不懂怎么我不还骂他,但那没有关系,不声不响并不就是善罢甘休。我要写一封辱骂的信给他,你可以给我带去。你肯不肯,西尔维斯?

西尔维斯 菲苾,那是我再愿意不过的了。

菲苾 我就写去。这件事情萦绕在我的心头,我要简简单单地把他挖苦一下。跟我去,西尔维斯。(同下)

第四幕

第一场
亚登森林

【罗瑟琳、西莉娅及杰奎斯上。

杰奎斯 可爱的少年,请你许我跟你结识结识。

罗瑟琳 他们说你是个多愁的人。

杰奎斯 是的,我喜欢发愁不喜欢笑。

罗瑟琳 这两件事各趋极端,都会叫人讨厌,比之醉汉更容易招一般人的指摘。

杰奎斯 发发愁不说话,有什么不好?

罗瑟琳 那么何不做一根木头呢?

杰奎斯 我没有读书人的那种争强斗胜的烦恼,也没有音乐家的那种胡思乱想的烦恼,也没有官员们的那种作威作福的烦恼,也没有军人们的那种侵权夺利的烦恼,也没有律师们的那种卖狡弄狯的烦恼,也没有姑娘家的那种吹毛求疵的烦恼,也没有情人们的这一切种种合拢来的烦恼。我的烦恼全然是我自己的,它是由各种成分组合而成,从许多事物中提炼出来,那是我们旅行中所得到的各种观感,因为不断沉思而使我充满了十分古怪的忧愁。

罗瑟琳 你是一个旅行家吗?噢,那你就有应该悲哀的理由了。我想你多半是卖去了自己的田地去看别人的田地,看见的这么多,自己却一无所有,眼睛是看饱了,两手却是空空的。

杰奎斯 是的,我已经得到了我的经验。

罗瑟琳 而你的经验使你悲哀。我宁愿叫一个傻瓜来逗我发笑,不愿叫经验来使我悲哀。而且还要到各处旅行去找它!

【奥兰多上。

奥兰多　早安,亲爱的罗瑟琳!

杰奎斯　你要念起诗来,那么我可要少陪了。(下)

罗瑟琳　再会,旅行家先生。你该打起些南腔北调,穿了些奇装异服,瞧不起本国的一切好处,厌恶你的故乡,简直要怨恨上帝干吗不给你生一副外国人的相貌;否则我可不能相信你曾经在威尼斯荡过艇子。——啊,怎么,奥兰多!你这些时候都在哪儿?你算是一个情人!要是你再对我来这么一套,你可再不用来见我了。

奥兰多　我的好罗瑟琳,我来得不过迟了一小时还不满。

罗瑟琳　误了一小时的情人的约会!谁要是把一分钟分作了一千分,而在恋爱上误了一千分之一分钟的几分之一的约会,这种人人家也许会说丘比特曾经拍过他的肩膀,可是我敢说他的心是不曾中过爱神之箭的。

奥兰多　原谅我吧,亲爱的罗瑟琳!

罗瑟琳　哼,要是你再这样慢吞吞的,以后不用再来见我了。我宁愿让一只蜗牛向我献殷勤。

奥兰多　一只蜗牛!

罗瑟琳　对了,一只蜗牛;因为它虽然走得慢,可是却把它的屋子顶在头上,我想这是一份比你所能给予一个女人的更好的家产,而且它还随身带着它的命运哩。

奥兰多　那是什么?

罗瑟琳　嘿,角儿哪,那正是你所要谢谢你的妻子的,可是他却自己随身带了它做武器,免得人家说他妻子的坏话。

奥兰多　贤德的女子不会叫她丈夫当王八,我的罗瑟琳是贤德的。

罗瑟琳　而我是你的罗瑟琳吗?

西莉娅　他喜欢这样叫你,可是他有一个长得比你漂亮的罗瑟琳哩。

罗瑟琳　来,向我求婚,向我求婚,我现在很高兴,多半会答应你。假如我真是你的罗瑟琳,你现在要向我说些什么话?

奥兰多　我要在没有说话之前先接个吻。

罗瑟琳　不,你最好先说话,等到所有的话都说完了,想不出什么来的时候,你就可以趁此接吻。善于演说的人,当他们一时无话可说之际,他们会吐一口痰;情人们呢,上帝保佑我们!倘使缺少了说话的资料,接吻是最便当的补救办法。

奥兰多　假如她不肯让我吻她呢?

罗瑟琳　那么她就使得你向她请求,这样又有了新的话题了。

奥兰多　谁见了他的心爱的情人而会说不出话来呢?

罗瑟琳　哼,假如我是你的情人,你就会说不出话来。我不是你的罗瑟琳吗?

奥兰多　我很愿意把你当作罗瑟琳,因为这样我就可以讲着她了。

罗瑟琳　好,我代表她说我不愿接受你。

奥兰多　那么我代表我自己说我要死去。

罗瑟琳　不,真的,还是请个人代死吧。这个可怜的世界差不多有六千年的岁数了,可是从来不曾有过一个人亲自殉情而死。特洛伊罗斯①是被一个希腊人的棍棒砸出了脑浆的,可是在这以前他就已经寻过死,而他是一个模范的情人。即使希罗当了尼姑,里昂德也会活下去活了好多年的,倘不是因为一个酷热的仲夏之夜,因为,好孩子,他本来只是要到赫勒斯滂海峡里去洗个澡的,可是在水中害起抽筋来,因而淹死了:那时代的愚蠢的史家却说他是为了塞斯托斯的希罗而死②。这些全都是谎。人们一代一代地死去,他们的尸体都给蛆虫吃了,可是绝不会为爱情而死的。

奥兰多　我不愿我的真正的罗瑟琳也做这样想法,因为我可以发誓说她只要皱一皱眉头就会把我杀死。

罗瑟琳　我凭着此手发誓,那是连一只苍蝇也杀不死的。

---

①　特洛伊罗斯(Troilus),莎翁传奇剧《特洛埃围城记》中的主角。

②　利昂特(Leander)与希罗(Hero)为希腊传说中的一对恋人名,利昂特每晚泅水过赫勒斯滂(Hellespont)以会其恋人,一夕大风浪没顶。

但是来吧,现在我要做你的一个乖乖的罗瑟琳,你向我要求什么,我一定应允你。

奥兰多　那么爱我吧,罗瑟琳!

罗瑟琳　好,我就爱你,星期五、星期六以及其他一切的日子。

奥兰多　你肯接受我吗?

罗瑟琳　肯的,我肯接受像你这样二十个男人。

奥兰多　你怎么说?

罗瑟琳　你不是个好人吗?

奥兰多　我希望是的。

罗瑟琳　那么好的东西会嫌太多吗?——来,妹妹,你要扮作牧师,给我们主婚。——把你的手给我,奥兰多。你怎么说,妹妹?

奥兰多　请你给我们主婚。

西莉娅　我不会说。

罗瑟琳　你应当这样开始:"奥兰多,你愿不愿——"

西莉娅　好吧。——奥兰多,你愿不愿娶这个罗瑟琳为妻?

奥兰多　我愿意。

罗瑟琳　嗯,但是什么时候才娶呢?

奥兰多　当然就在现在哪。只要她能替我们完成婚礼。

罗瑟琳　那么你必须说:"罗瑟琳,我娶你为妻。"

奥兰多　罗瑟琳,我娶你为妻。

罗瑟琳　我本来可以问你凭着什么来娶我的,可是奥兰多,我愿意接受你做我的丈夫。——这丫头等不到牧师问起,就冲口说了出来了。真的,女人的思想总是比行动跑得更快。

奥兰多 一切的思想都是这样,它们是生着翅膀的。

罗瑟琳 现在你告诉我你占有了她之后,打算保留到多久?

奥兰多 永久再加上一天。

罗瑟琳 说一天,不用说永久。不,不,奥兰多,男人们在未婚的时候是四月天,结婚的时候是十二月天;姑娘们做姑娘的时候是五月天,一做了妻子,季候便改变了。我要比一头巴巴里雄鸽对待它的雌鸽格外多疑地对待你,我要比下雨前的鹦鹉格外吵闹,比猢狲格外弃旧怜新,比猴子格外反复无常;我要在你高兴的时候像喷泉上的狄安娜女神雕像一样无端哭泣,我要在你想睡的时候像土狼一样纵声大笑。

奥兰多 但是我的罗瑟琳会做出这种事来吗?

罗瑟琳 我可以发誓她会像我一样做出来的。

奥兰多 啊!但是她是个聪明人哩。

罗瑟琳 她倘不聪明,怎么有本领做这等事?越是聪明,越是淘气。假如用一扇门把一个女人的才情关起来,它会从窗子里钻出来的;关了窗,它会从钥匙孔里钻出来的;塞住了钥匙孔,它会跟着一道烟从烟囱里飞出来的。

奥兰多 男人娶到了这种有才情的老婆,就难免要感慨"才情才情,看你横行到什么地方"了。

罗瑟琳 不,你可以把那句骂人的话留起来,等你瞧见你妻子的才情爬到你邻人的床上去的时候再说。

奥兰多 那时这位多才的妻子又将用怎样的才情来辩解呢?

罗瑟琳 呃,她会说她是到那儿找你去的。你捉住她,她总有话好说,除非你把她的舌头割掉。唉!要是一个女人不会把她的错处推到她男人的身上去,那种女人千万不要让她抚养她自己的孩子,因为她会把他抚养得成为一个傻子的。

奥兰多 罗瑟琳,这两小时我要离开你。

罗瑟琳 唉!爱人,我两小时都缺不了你哪。

奥兰多 我一定要陪公爵吃饭去。到两点钟我就会回来。

罗瑟琳 好,你去吧,你去吧!我知道你会变成怎样的人。我的朋友们这样对我说过,我也这样相信着,你是用你那种花言巧语来把我骗上手的。不过又是一个给人丢弃的罢了。好,死就死吧!你是说两点钟吗?

奥兰多 是的,亲爱的罗瑟琳。

罗瑟琳 凭着良心,一本正经,上帝保佑我,我可以向你起一切无关紧要的誓,要是你失了一点点儿的约,或是比约定的时间来迟了一分钟,我就要把你当作一大堆无义的人中间一个最可怜的背信者、最空心的情人,最不配被你叫作罗瑟琳的那人所爱的。所以,留心我的责骂,守你的约吧。

奥兰多 我一定恪遵,就像你真是我的罗瑟琳一样。好,再见。

罗瑟琳 好,时间是审判一切这一类罪人的老法官,让他来审判吧。再见。(奥兰多下)

西莉娅 你在你那种情话中间简直是侮辱我们女性。我们一定要把你的衫裤揭到你的头上,让全世界的人看看鸟儿怎样作践了她自己的窠。

罗瑟琳 啊,小妹妹,小妹妹,我的可爱的小妹妹,你要知道我是爱得多么深!可是我的爱是无从测计深度的,因为它有一个渊深莫测的底,像葡萄牙海湾一样。

西莉娅 或者不如说是没有底的吧,你刚把你的爱倒进去,它就漏了出来。

罗瑟琳 不,维纳斯的那个坏蛋私生子①,那个因为忧郁而感孕,因为冲动而受胎,因为疯狂而诞生的那个瞎眼的坏孩子,因为自己没有眼睛而把每个人的眼睛都欺蒙了的,让他来判断我爱得多么深吧。我告诉你,爱莲娜,我不看见奥兰多便活不下去。我要找一处树荫,到那儿长吁短叹地等着他回来。

西莉娅 我要去睡一个觉。(同下)

---

① 指丘比特。

第二场
林中的另一部分

【杰奎斯、众臣及林居人等上。

杰奎斯　是谁把鹿杀死的?

臣甲　先生,是我。

杰奎斯　让我们引他去见公爵,像一个罗马的凯旋将军一样。顶好把鹿角插在他头上,表示胜利的光荣。林居人,你们没有个应景的歌儿吗?

林居人 有的,先生。

杰奎斯 那么唱起来吧,不要管他调子怎样,只要可以热闹热闹就是了。

林居人 (唱)

  杀鹿的人好幸福,
  穿它的皮顶它角。
   唱个歌儿送送他。(众和)
  顶了鹿角莫讥笑,
  古时便已当冠帽;
   你的祖父戴过它,
   你的阿爹顶过它,
  鹿角鹿角壮而美,
  你们取笑真不对。(众下)

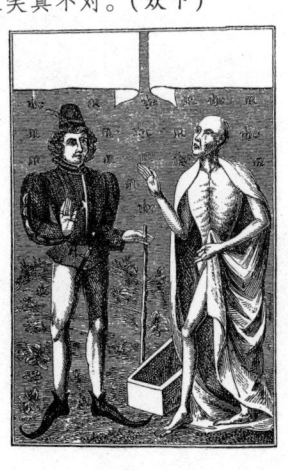

第三场
林中的另一部分

【罗瑟琳及西莉娅上。

罗瑟琳 你现在怎么说?不是过了两点钟了吗?这儿有什么奥兰多!

西莉娅 我对你说,他怀着纯洁的爱情和忧虑的头脑,带了弓箭出去睡觉了。瞧,谁来了。

【西尔维斯上。

西尔维斯 我奉命来见您,美貌的少年。我的温柔的菲苾要我把这信送给您。(将信交罗瑟琳)里面说的什么话我不知道,但是照她写这封信的时候那发怒的神气看来,多半是一些气恼的话。原谅我,我只是个不知情的送信人。

罗瑟琳 (阅信)最有耐性的人见了这封信也要暴跳如雷;是可忍,孰不可忍!她说我不漂亮,说我没有礼貌,说我骄傲,说即使男人像凤凰那样稀罕,她也不会爱我。天哪!我并不曾要追求她的爱,她为什么写这种话给我呢?好,牧人,好,这封信是你捣的鬼。

西尔维斯 不,我发誓我不知道里面写些什么,这封信是菲苾写的。

罗瑟琳 算了吧,算了吧,你是个傻瓜,为了爱情颠倒到这等地步。我看见过她的手,她的手就像一块牛皮那样粗糙,有着沙石那样的颜色,我以为她戴着一副旧手套,哪知道原来就是她的手,她有一双做粗工的手,但这可不用管他。我说她从来不承想到过写这封信,这是男人出的花样,是一个男人的笔迹。

西尔维斯 真的,那是她的笔迹。

罗瑟琳 嘿,这是粗暴的凶狠的口气,全然是挑战的口气,嘿,她就像土耳其人向基督徒那样向我挑战呢。女人家的温柔的头脑里,绝不会想出这种恣睢暴戾的念头来,这种狠恶的字句,含着比字面更狠恶的用意。你要不要听听这封信?

西尔维斯 假如您愿意,请您念给我听听吧。因为我还不曾听到过它呢,虽然关于菲苾的凶狠的话,倒已经听了不少了。

罗瑟琳 她要向我撒野呢。听那只雌老虎怎样写法:(读)
　　你是不是天神的化身,
　　来燃烧一个少女的心?
女人会这样骂人吗?

西尔维斯 您把这种话叫作骂人吗?

罗瑟琳 (读)
　　撇下了你神圣的殿堂,
　　虐弄一个痴心的姑娘?

你听见过这种骂人的话吗?

　　人们的眼睛向我求爱,

　　从不曾给我丝毫损害。

意思说我是个畜生。

　　你一双美目中的轻蔑,

　　尚能勾起我这般情热;

　　唉!假如你能青眼相加,

　　我更将怎样意乱如麻!

　　你一边骂,我一边爱你;

　　你倘求我,我何事不依?

　　代我传达情意的来使,

　　并不知道我这段心事;

　　让他带下了你的回报,

　　告诉我你的青春年少,

　　肯不肯接受我的奉献,

　　把我的一切听你调遣;

　　否则就请把拒绝明言,

　　我准备一死了却情缘。

西尔维斯　您把这叫作骂吗?

西莉娅　唉,可怜的牧人!

罗瑟琳　你可怜他吗?不,他是不值得怜悯的。你会爱这种女人吗?嘿,利用你做工具,那样玩弄你!怎么受得住!好,你到她那儿去吧,因为我知道爱情已经把你变成一条驯服的蛇了。你去对她说：要是她爱我，我吩咐她爱你；要是她不肯爱你，那么我决不要她，除非你代她恳求。假如你是个真心的恋人，去吧，别说一句话。瞧，又有人来了。（西尔维斯下）

【奥列佛上。

奥列佛 早安，两位。请问你们知不知道在这座树林的边界有一所用橄榄树围绕着的羊栏？

西莉娅 在这儿的西面，附近的山谷之下，从那微语喃喃的泉水旁边那一列柳树的地方向右出发，便可以到那边去。但现在那边只有一所空屋，没有人在里面。

奥列佛 假如听了人家嘴里的叙述便可以用眼睛认识出来，那么你们的模样正是我所听到说起的，穿着这样的衣服，这样的年纪："那少年生得很俊，脸孔像个女人，行为举动像是老大姊似的；那女人是矮矮的，比她的哥哥黝黑些。"你们正是我所要寻访的那屋子的主人吗？

西莉娅 既蒙下问，那么我们说我们正是那屋子的主人，也不算是自己的夸口了。

奥列佛 奥兰多要我向你们两位致意；这一方染着血迹的手帕，他叫我送给他称为他的罗瑟琳的那位少年。您就是他吗？

罗瑟琳 正是。这是什么意思呢？

奥列佛 说起来徒增我的惭愧，假如你们要知道我是谁，这一方手帕怎样、为什么、在哪里沾上这些血迹。

西莉娅　请您说吧。

奥列佛　年轻的奥兰多上次跟你们分别的时候,曾经答应过在一小时之内回来。他正在林中走过,品味着爱情的甜蜜和苦涩,瞧,什么事发生了!他把眼睛向旁边一望,他好像看见了些什么东西:在一株满覆着苍苔的秃顶的老橡树之下,有一个不幸的衣衫褴褛须发蓬松的人仰面睡着。一条金绿的蛇缠在他的头上,正预备把它的头敏捷地伸进他的张开的嘴里去,可是突然看见了奥兰多,它便松了开来,蜿蜒地溜进林莽中去了。在那林荫下有一头乳房干瘪的母狮,头贴着地蹲伏着,像猫一样注视这睡着的人的动静,因为那畜生有一种高贵的素性,不会去侵犯瞧上去似乎已经死了的东西。奥兰多一见了这情形,便走到那人的面前,一看却是他的兄长,他的大哥。

西莉娅　啊!我听他说起过那个哥哥,他说他是一个再忍心伤天害理不过的。

奥列佛　他很可以那样说,因为我知道他确是忍心伤天害理的。

罗瑟琳　但是我们说奥兰多吧。他把他丢下在那儿,让他给那饿狮吃了吗?

奥列佛　他两次转身想去,可是善心比复仇更高贵,天性克服了他的私怨,使他去和那母狮格斗,很快地那狮子便向他扑了上来。我听见了搏击的声音,就从苦恼的瞌睡中醒过来了。

西莉娅　你就是他的哥哥吗?

罗瑟琳　他救的便是你吗?

西莉娅　老是设计谋害他的便是你吗?

奥列佛　那是从前的我,不是现在的我。我现在已经变成个新的人了,因此我可以不惭愧地告诉你们我从前的为人。

罗瑟琳　可是那块血渍的手帕是怎样来的?

奥列佛　别性急。那时我们两人叙述着彼此的经历,以及我到这荒野里来的原委,一面说一面自然流露的眼泪流个不住。简单地说,他把我领去见那善良的公爵,公爵赏给我新衣服穿,款待着我,吩咐我的弟弟照应我。于是他立刻带我到他的洞里去,脱下衣服来,一看臂上给母狮抓去了一块肉,血不停地流着,那时他便晕了过去,嘴里还念着罗瑟琳的名字。简单地说,我把他救醒转来,裹好了他的伤口。略过些时,他精神恢复了,便叫我这个陌生人到这儿来把这件事通知你们,请你们原谅他的失约。这一方手帕在他的血里浸过,他要我交给他戏称为罗瑟琳的那位青年牧人。(罗瑟琳晕去。)

西莉娅　呀,怎么啦,盖尼米德! 亲爱的盖尼米德!

奥列佛　有好多人一见了血便要发晕。

西莉娅　还有其他的缘故哩。哥哥! 盖尼米德!

奥列佛　瞧,他醒过来了。

罗瑟琳　我要回家去。

西莉娅　我们可以陪着你去。——请您扶着他的臂膀好不好?

奥列佛　提起精神来,孩子。你算是个男人吗?你太没有男人气了。

罗瑟琳　一点不错,我承认。啊,好小子!人家会觉得我假装得很像哩。请您告诉令弟我假装得多么像。哎哟!

奥列佛　这不是假装,你的脸色已经有了太清楚的证明,这是出于真情的。

罗瑟琳　告诉您吧,真的是假装的。

罗瑟琳 我正在假装着呢,可是凭良心说,我理该是个女人。

西莉娅 来,你瞧上去脸色越变越白了,回家去吧。好先生,陪我们去吧。

奥列佛 好的,因为我必须把你怎样原谅舍弟的回音带回去呢,罗瑟琳。

罗瑟琳 我会想出些什么来的。但是我请您就把我的假装的样子告诉他吧。我们走吧。(同下)

第五幕

第一场
亚登森林

【试金石及奥德蕾上。

试金石　咱们总会找到一个时间的,奥德蕾,耐心点儿吧,温柔的奥德蕾。

奥德蕾　那位老先生虽然这么说,其实这个牧师也很好呀。

试金石　顶坏不过的奥列佛师傅,奥德蕾;顶不好的马坦克斯特。但是,奥德蕾,林子里有一个年轻人要向你求婚呢。

奥德蕾　嗯,我知道他是谁,他跟我全没有关涉。你说起的那个人来了。

【威廉上。

试金石　看见一个村汉在我是家常便饭。凭良心说话,我们这辈聪明人真是作孽不浅,我们总是忍不住要寻寻人家的开心。

威廉　晚安,奥德蕾。

奥德蕾 你晚安哪,威廉。

威廉 晚安,先生。

试金石 晚安,好朋友。把帽子戴上了,把帽子戴上了,请不用客气,把帽子戴上了。你多大年纪了,朋友?

威廉 二十五了,先生。

试金石 正是妙龄。你名叫威廉吗?

威廉 威廉,先生。

试金石 一个好名字。是生在这林子里的吗?

威廉 是的,先生,我感谢上帝。

试金石 "感谢上帝",很好的回答。很有钱吗?

威廉 呃,先生,不过如此。

试金石 "不过如此",很好很好,好得很。可是也不算怎么好,不过如此而已。你聪明吗?

威廉 呃,先生,我还算聪明。

试金石 啊,你说得很好。我现在记起一句话来了:"傻子自以为聪明,但聪明人知道他自己是个傻子。"异教的哲学家想要吃一颗葡萄的时候,便张开嘴唇来,把它放进嘴里去,那意思是表示葡萄是生下来给人吃,嘴唇是生下来要张开的。你爱这姑娘吗?

威廉 是的,先生。

试金石 把你的手给我。你有学问吗?

威廉 没有,先生。

试金石 那么让我教训你:有者有也。修辞学上有这么一个比喻,把酒从杯子里倒在碗里,一只满了,那一只便要落空。写文章的人大家都承认"彼"即是他。好,你不是彼,因为我是他。

威廉 哪一个他,先生?

试金石 先生,就是要跟这个女人结婚的他。所以,你这村夫,莫——那在俗话里就是不要——与此妇——那在土话里就是和这个女人——交游——那在普通话里就是来往,合拢来说,莫与此妇交游,否则,村夫,你就要毁灭。或者让你容易明白些,你就要死,那就是说,我要杀死你,把你干掉,叫你活不成,让你当奴才。我要用毒药毒死你,一顿棒儿打死你,或者用钢刀搠死你;我要跟你打架;我要想出计策来打倒你;我要用一百五十种法子杀死你。所以赶快发着抖滚吧。

奥德蕾 你快去吧,好威廉。

威廉 上帝保佑您快活,先生。(下)

【柯林上。

柯林 我们的大官人和小娘子找着你哪。来,走啊!走啊!

试金石 走,奥德蕾!走,奥德蕾!我就来,我就来。(同下)

第二场
林中的另一部分

【奥兰多及奥列佛上。

奥兰多 你跟她相识得这么浅便会喜欢起她来了吗?一看见了她,便会爱起她来了吗?一爱了她,便会求起婚来了吗?一求了婚,她便会答应你吗?你一定要得到她吗?

奥列佛 这件事进行的匆促,她的贫穷,相识的不久,我的突然的求婚和她的突然的应允,这些你都不用怀疑,只要你承认我是爱着爱莲娜的,承认她是爱着我的,允许我们两人结合。这样你也会有好处,因为我愿意把我父亲老罗兰爵士的房屋和一切收入都让给你,我自己在这里终生做一个牧人。

奥兰多 你可以得到我的允许。你们的婚礼就在明天举行吧,我可以去把公爵和他的一切乐天的从者都请来。你去吩咐爱莲娜预备一切。瞧,我的罗瑟琳来了。

【罗瑟琳上。

罗瑟琳 上帝保佑你,哥哥。

奥列佛 也保佑你,好妹妹。(下)

罗瑟琳 啊!我的亲爱的奥兰多,我瞧见你把你的心裹在绷带里,我是多么难过呀。

奥兰多 那是我的臂膀。

罗瑟琳 我以为是你的心给狮子抓伤了。

奥兰多 它的确是受了伤,但却是给一位姑娘的眼睛伤害了的。

罗瑟琳 你的哥哥有没有告诉你当他把你的手帕给我看的时候,我假装晕去了的情形?

奥兰多 是的,而且还有更奇怪的事情呢。

罗瑟琳 噢!我知道你说的是什么。噢,那倒是真的。从来不曾有过这么快的事情,除了两只公羊的打架和恺撒那句"我来过,我看见,我征服"的傲语①。令兄和舍妹刚见了面,便大家瞧起来了,一瞧便相爱了;一相爱便叹气了;一叹气便彼此问为的是什么;一知道了为的是什么,便要想补救的办法:这样一步一步地踏到了结婚的阶段,不久他们便要成其好事了,否则他们等不到结婚便要放肆起来的。他们简直爱得慌了,一定要在一块儿,用棒儿也打不散他们。

奥兰多 他们明天便要成婚,我就要去请公爵参加婚礼。但是,唉!从别人的眼中看见幸福,多么令人烦闷。明天我越是想到我的哥哥满足了心愿多么快活,我便将

---

① Veni, vidi, vici (I came, I saw, I conquered),为恺撒(Julius Caesar)征服 Pontus 王 Pharnaces 后告知罗马贵族院之有名豪语。

越是伤心。

罗瑟琳　难道我明天不能仍旧充作你的罗瑟琳吗?

奥兰多　我不能老是靠着幻想而生存了。

罗瑟琳　那么我不再用空话来叫你心烦了。告诉你吧,现在我不是说着玩儿,我知道你是一个有见识的上等人,我并不是因为希望你赞美我的本领而恭维你,我要使你相信我的话,也不是图自己的名气,只是为着你的好处。假如你肯相信,那么我告诉你,我会行奇迹。从三岁时起我就和一个术士结识,他的法术非常高深,可是并不作恶害人。要是你爱罗瑟琳真是爱得那么深,就像你瞧上去的那样,那么你哥哥和爱莲娜结婚的时候,你就可以和她结婚。我知道她现在的处境是多么不幸,只要你没有什么不方便,我一定能够明天叫她亲身出现在你的面前,一点没有危险。

奥兰多　你说的是真话吗?

罗瑟琳　我以生命为誓,我说的是真话。虽然我说我是个术士,可是我很重视我的生命呢。所以你得穿上你最好的衣服,邀请你的朋友们来,只要你愿意在明天结婚,你一定可以结婚,和罗瑟琳结婚,要是你愿意。瞧,我的一个爱人和她的一个爱人来了。

【西尔维斯及菲苾上。

菲苾　少年人,你很对我不起,把我写给你的信宣布了出来。

罗瑟琳 要是我把它宣布了,我也不管;我存心要对你傲慢不客气。你背后跟着一个忠心的牧人。瞧着他吧,爱他吧,他崇拜着你哩。

菲芯 好牧人,告诉这个少年人恋爱是怎样的。

西尔维斯 它是充满了叹息和眼泪的。我正是这样爱着菲芯。

菲芯 我也是这样爱着盖尼米德。

奥兰多 我也是这样爱着罗瑟琳。

罗瑟琳 我可是一个女人也不爱。

西尔维斯 它是全然的忠心和服务。我正是这样爱着菲芯。

菲芯 我也是这样爱着盖尼米德。

奥兰多 我也是这样爱着罗瑟琳。

罗瑟琳 我可是一个女人也不爱。

西尔维斯 它是全然的空想,全然的热情,全然的愿望,全然的崇拜、恭顺和尊敬;全然的谦卑,全然的忍耐和焦心;全然的纯洁,全然的磨炼。我正是这样爱着菲芯。

菲芯 我也是这样爱着盖尼米德。

奥兰多 我也是这样爱着罗瑟琳。

罗瑟琳 我可是一个女人也不爱。

菲芯 (向罗瑟琳)假如真是这样,那么你为什么责备我爱你呢?

西尔维斯 (向菲芯)假如真是这样,那么你为什么责备我爱你呢?

奥兰多 假如真是这样,那么你为什么责备我爱你呢?

罗瑟琳 你在向谁说话——"你为什么责备我爱你呢"?

奥兰多 向那不在这里,也听不见我的说话的她。

罗瑟琳 请你们别再说下去了吧,这简直像是一群爱尔兰的狼向着月亮嗥叫。(向西尔维斯)要是我能够,我一定帮助你。(向菲苾)要是我有可能,我一定会爱你。明天大家来和我相会。(向菲苾)假如我会跟女人结婚,我一定跟你结婚;我要在明天结婚了。(向奥兰多)假如我会使男人满足,我一定使你满足;你要在明天结婚了。(向西尔维斯)假如使你喜欢的东西能使你满

意,我一定使你满意;你要在明天结婚了。(向奥兰多)你既然爱罗瑟琳,请你赴约。(向西尔维斯)你既然爱菲苾,请你赴约。我既然不爱什么女人,我也赴约。现在再见吧。我已经吩咐过你们了。

西尔维斯 只要我活着,我一定不失约。

菲苾 我也不失约。

奥兰多 我也不失约。(各下)

第三场
林中的另一部分

【试金石及奥德蕾上。

试金石 明天是快乐的好日子,奥德蕾,明天我们要结婚了。

奥德蕾 我满心盼望着呢;我希望盼望出嫁并不是一个不正当的愿望。有两个放逐的公爵的童儿来了。

【二童上。

童甲 遇见得巧啊,好先生。

试金石 巧得很,巧得很。来,请坐,请坐,唱个歌儿。

童乙 遵命遵命。居中坐下吧。

童甲 一副坏喉咙未唱之前,总少不了来些老套子,例如咳嗽吐痰或是说嗓子有点儿哑了之类。我们还是免了这些,马上唱起来怎样?
童乙 好的,好的。两人齐声同唱,就像两个吉卜赛人骑在一匹马上。

歌

一对情人并着肩,
哎哟哎哟哎哎哟,
走过了青青稻麦田,
　春天是最好的结婚天,
听嘤嘤歌唱枝头鸟,
　姐郎们最爱春光好。

小麦青青大麦鲜,
　哎哟哎哟哎哎哟,
乡女村男交颈儿眠,
　春天是最好的结婚天云云。
新歌一曲意缠绵,
　哎哟哎哟哎哎哟,
人生美满像好花妍,
　春天是最好的结婚天云云。

劝君莫负艳阳天,
　哎哟哎哟哎哎哟,
恩爱欢娱要趁少年

春天是最好的结婚天云云。

试金石　老实说,年轻的先生们,这首歌词固然没有多大意思,那调子却也很不入调。

童甲　您弄错了,先生。我们是照着板眼唱的,一拍也没有漏过。

试金石　凭良心说,我来听这么一首傻气的歌儿,真算是白糟蹋了时间。上帝和你们同在,上帝把你们的喉咙补补好吧!来,奥德蕾。(各下)

第四场
林中的另一部分

【老公爵、阿米恩斯、杰奎斯、奥兰多、奥列佛及西莉娅同上。

公爵 奥兰多,你相信那孩子果真有他所说的那种本领吗?

奥兰多 我有时相信,有时不相信,就像那些因恐结果无望而心中惴惴的人,一面希望一面担着心事。

【罗瑟琳、西尔维斯及菲苾上。

罗瑟琳 再请耐心听我说一遍我们所约定的条件。(向公爵)您不是说,假如我把您的罗瑟琳带了来,您愿意把她赏给这位奥兰多做妻子吗?

公爵 即使再要我把几个王国作为陪嫁,我也愿意。

罗瑟琳 (向奥兰多)您不是说,假如我带了她来,您愿意娶她吗?

奥兰多 即使我是统治万国的君王,我也愿意。

罗瑟琳 (向菲苾)您不是说,假如我愿意,您便愿意嫁我吗?

菲苾 即使我在一小时后就要一命丧亡,我也愿意。

罗瑟琳 但是假如您不愿意嫁我,您不是要嫁给这位忠心无比的牧人吗?

菲苾　是这样约定着。

罗瑟琳　(向西尔维斯)您不是说,假如菲苾愿意,您便愿意娶她吗?

西尔维斯　即使娶了她等于送死,我也愿意。

罗瑟琳　我答应要把这一切事情安排得好好的。公爵,请您守约许嫁您的女儿;奥兰多,请您守约娶他的女儿;菲苾,请您守约嫁我,假如不肯嫁我,便得嫁给这位牧人;西尔维斯,请您守约娶她,假如她不肯嫁我。现在我就去给你们解释这些疑惑。(罗瑟琳、西莉娅下)

公爵　这个牧童使我记起了我的女儿的相貌,有几分活像是她。

奥兰多　殿下,我初次见他的时候,也以为他是郡主的兄弟呢。但是,殿下,这孩子是在林中生长的,他的伯父曾经教过他一些魔术的原理,据说他那伯父是一个隐居在这儿林中的大术士。

【试金石及奥德蕾上。

杰奎斯　一定又有一次洪水来啦,这一对一对都要准备躲到方舟里去①。又来了一对奇怪的畜生,傻瓜是他们公认的名字。

试金石　列位,这厢有礼了!

杰奎斯　殿下,请您欢迎他。这就是我在林中常常遇见的

---

① 指创世记中洪水时诺亚造方舟之事。

113

那位傻头傻脑的先生；据他说他还出入过宫廷呢。

试金石 要是有人不相信，尽管把我质问好了。我曾经跳过高雅的舞；我曾经恭维过一位贵妇；我曾经向我的朋友弄过手腕，跟我的仇家们装亲热；我曾经毁了三个裁缝，闹过四回口角，有一次几乎打出手。

杰奎斯 那是怎样闹起来的呢？

试金石 呃，我们碰见了，一查这场争吵是根据着第七个原因。

杰奎斯 怎么叫第七个原因？——殿下，请您喜欢这个家伙。

公爵 我很喜欢他。

试金石 上帝保佑您，殿下。我希望您喜欢我。殿下，我挤在这一对对乡村的姐儿郎儿中间到这里来，也是想来宣了誓然后毁誓，让婚姻把我们结合，再让血气把我们拆开。她是个寒碜的姑娘，殿下，样子又难看；可是，殿下，她是我自个儿的。我有一个坏脾气，殿下，人家不要的我偏要。宝贵的贞洁，殿下，就像是住在破屋子里的守财奴，又像是丑蚌壳里的明珠。

公爵 我说，他倒很伶俐机警呢。

杰奎斯 但是且说那第七个原因。你怎么知道这场争吵是根据着第七个原因呢？

试金石 因为那是根据着一句经过七次演变后的谎话。——把你的身体站端正些，奥德蕾。——是这样的,先生:我不喜欢某位廷臣的胡须的式样;他回我说假如我说他的胡须的式样不好,他却自以为很好,这叫作"有礼的驳斥"。假如我再去对他说那式样不好,他就回我说他自己喜欢要这样,这叫作"谦恭的讥刺"。要是再说那式样不好,他便蔑视我的意见,这叫作"粗暴的答复"。要是再说那式样不好,他就回答说我讲得不对,这叫作"大胆的谴责"。要是再说那式样不好,他就要说我说谎,这叫作"挑衅的反攻"。于是就到了"委婉的说谎"和"公然的说谎"。

杰奎斯 你说了几次他的胡须式样不好呢?

试金石 我只敢说到"委婉的说谎"为止,他也不敢给我"公然的说谎"。因此我们较了较剑,便走开了。

杰奎斯 你能不能把一句谎话的各种程度按着次序说出来?

试金石 先生啊,我们争吵都是根据着书本的,就像你们有讲礼貌的书一样。我可以把各种程度列举出来。第一,有礼的驳斥;第二,谦恭的讥刺;第三,粗暴的答复;第四,大胆的谴责;第五,挑衅的反攻;第六,委婉的说谎;第七,公然的说谎。除了"公然的说谎"之外,其余的都可以避免,但是"公然的说谎"只要用了"假如"两个字,也就可以一天云散。我知道有一场七个法官都处断不了的争吵,当两边相遇时,其中的一个单单想起了"假如"两字,例如"假如你这样说,那么我便要这样说",于是两人便彼此握手,结为兄弟了。"假如"是唯一的和事佬;"假如"之时用大矣哉!

杰奎斯 殿下,这不是一个很难得的人吗?他什么都懂,然而仍然是一个傻瓜。

公爵 他把他的傻气当作了藏身的烟幕,在它的荫蔽之下放出他的机智来。

【许门领罗瑟琳穿女装及西莉娅上。柔和的音乐。

许门 天上有喜气融融,
　　　人间万事尽亨通,
　　　　和合无嫌猜。
　　　公爵,接受你女儿,
　　　亥门一路带着伊,
　　　　远从天上来;
　　　请你为她作主张,
　　　嫁给她心上情郎。

罗瑟琳 (向公爵)我把我自己交给您,因为我是您的。(向奥兰多)我把我自己交给您,因为我是您的。

公爵 要是眼前所见的并不是虚假,那么你是我的女儿了。

奥兰多 要是眼前所见的并不是虚假,那么你是我的罗瑟琳了。

菲苾 要是眼前的情形是真,那么永别了,我的爱人!

罗瑟琳 (向公爵)要是您不是我的父亲,那么我不要有什么父亲;(向奥兰多)要是您不是我的丈夫,那么我不要有什么丈夫;(向菲苾)要是我不跟你结婚,那么我再不跟别的女人结婚。

许门　请不要喧闹纷纷!
　　　这种种古怪事情,
　　　都得让许门断清。
　　　这里有四对恋人,
　　　说的话儿倘应心,
　　　该携手共缔鸳盟。
　　　你俩患难不相弃,(向奥兰多、罗瑟琳)
　　　你们俩同心永系;(向奥列佛、西莉娅)
　　　你和他宜室宜家,(向菲苾)
　　　再莫恋镜里空花;
　　　你两人形影相从,(向试金石、奥德蕾)
　　　像风雪跟着严冬。
　　　等一曲婚歌奏起,
　　　尽你们寻根觅底,
　　　莫惊讶咄咄怪事,
　　　细想想原来如此。

歌

人间添美眷,
　天后爱团圆;
席上同心侣,
　枕边并蒂莲。

> 不有亥门力,
>> 何缘众庶生?
> 同声齐赞颂,
>> 月老最堪称!

公爵 啊,我的亲爱的侄女!我欢迎你,就像你是我自己的女儿。

菲苾 (向西尔维斯)我不愿食言,现在你已经是我的,你的忠心使我爱上了你。

【贾奎斯上。

贾奎斯 请听我说一两句话,我是老罗兰爵士的第二个儿子,特意带了消息到这群贤毕集的地方来。弗莱德里克公爵因为听见每天有才智之士投奔到这林中,故此兴起大军,亲自统率,预备前来捉拿他的兄长,把他杀死除害。他到了这座树林的边界,遇见了一位高年的修道士,交谈之下,悔悟前非,便即停止进兵;同时看破红尘,把他的权位归还给他的被放逐的兄长,一同流亡在外的诸人的土地,也都各还原主。这不是假话,我可以用生命做担保。

公爵 欢迎,年轻人!你给你的兄弟们送了很好的新婚贺礼来了:一个是他的被扣押的土地;一个是一座绝大的公国,享有着绝对的主权。先让我们在这林中把我们已经在进行得好好的事情办了;然后,在这幸运的一群中,每一个曾经跟着我忍受过艰辛的日子的人,都要按着各人的地位,分享我的恢复了的荣华。现在我们且把这种新近得来的尊荣暂时搁在脑后,举行起我们乡村的狂欢来吧。奏起来,音乐!你们各位新娘新郎,大家欢天喜地的,跳起舞来呀!

杰奎斯 先生,恕我冒昧。要是我没有听错,好像您说的是那公爵已经潜心修道,抛弃富贵的宫廷了?

贾奎斯 是的。

杰奎斯 我就找他去,从这种悟道者的地方,很可以得到一些绝妙的教训。(向公爵)我让你去享受你那从前的光荣;那是你的忍耐和德行的酬报。(向奥兰多)你去享受你那用忠心赢得的爱情吧。(向奥列佛)你去享有你的土地、爱人和权势吧。(向西尔维斯)你去享用你那用千辛万苦换来的老婆吧。(向试金石)至于你呢,我让你去口角吧,因为在你的爱情的旅程上,你只带了两个月的粮草。好,大家各人去找各人的快乐;跳舞可不是我的份。

公爵 别走,杰奎斯,别走!

杰奎斯 我不想看你们的作乐;你们将会得到些什么,我就在被你们遗弃了的山窟中也可以知道的。(下)

公爵 进行下去吧,开始我们的嘉礼,自始至终谁都是满心的欢喜。(跳舞。众下)

收 场 白

罗瑟琳 叫娘儿们来念收场白,似乎不大合适,可是那也不见得比叫老爷子来念开场白更不成样子些。要是好酒无须招牌,那么好戏也不必有收场白;可是好酒要用好招牌,好戏倘再加上一段好收场白,岂不更好?那么我现在的情形是怎样的呢?既然不会念一段好收场白,又不能用一出好戏来讨好你们!我并不穿着得像个叫花子一样,因此我不能向你们求乞;我的唯一的法子是恳请。我要先从女人们着手。女人们啊!为着你们对于男子的爱情,请你们尽量地喜欢这本戏。男人们啊!为着你们对于女子的爱情——瞧你们那副痴笑的神气,我就知道你们没有一个讨厌她们的——请你们学着女人们的样子,也来喜欢这本戏。假如我是一个女人①,你们中间只要谁的胡子生得叫我满意,脸蛋长得讨我欢喜,而且气息也不叫我恶心的,我都愿意给他一吻。为了我这种慷慨的奉献,我相信凡是生得一副好胡子、长得一张好脸蛋或是有一口好气息的诸君,当我屈膝致敬的时候,都会向我道别。(下)

---

① 伊丽莎白时代舞台上女角皆用男童扮演。

AS YOU LIKE IT

Characters

DUKE	living in exile
FREDERICK	his brother, and usurper of his dominions
AMIENS	lord attending on the banished Duke
JAQUES	lord attending on the banished Duke
LE BEAU	a courtier attending upon Frederick
CHARLES	wrestler to Frederick
OLIVER	son of Sir Rowland de Boys
JAQUES	son of Sir Rowland de Boys
ORLANDO	son of Sir Rowland de Boys
ADAM	servant to Oliver
DENNIS	servant to Oliver
TOUCHSTONE	the court jester
SIR OLIVER MARTEXT	a vicar
CORIN	shepherd
SILVIUS	shepherd
WILLIAM	a country fellow, in love with Audrey
	A person representing HYMEN
ROSALIND	daughter to the banished Duke
CELIA	daughter to Frederick
PHEBE	a shepherdess
AUDREY	a country wench

Lords, Pages, Foresters, and Attendants

SCENE

OLIVER'S house; FREDERICK'S court; and the Forest of Arden

ACT1.

SCENE I.
Orchard of OLIVER'S house

[*Enter ORLANDO and ADAM*]

ORLANDO:

As I remember, Adam, it was upon this fashion bequeathed me by will but poor a thousand crowns, and, as thousay'st, charged my brother, on his blessing, to breed me well; and there begins my sadness. My brotherJaques he keeps at school, and report speaks goldenly of his profit. For my part, he keeps me rustically at home, or, to speak more properly, stays me here at homeunkept; for call you that keeping for a gentleman of my birth that differs not from the stalling of an ox? His horses are bred better; for, besides that they are fair with their feeding, they are taught their manage, and to that end riders dearly hir'd; but I, his brother, gain nothing under him but growth; for the which his animals on his dunghills are as much bound to him as I. Besides this nothing that he so plentifully gives me, the something that nature gave me his countenance seems to take from me. He lets me feed with his hinds, bars me the place of a brother, and as much as in him lies, mines my gentility with my education. This is it, Adam, that grieves me; and the spirit of my father, which I think is within me, begins to mutiny against this servitude. I will no longer endure it, though yet I know no wise remedy how to avoid it.

[*Enter OLIVER*]

ADAM:

Yonder comes my master, your brother.

ORLANDO:

Go apart, Adam, and thoushalt hear how he will shake me up.

[*ADAM retires*]

OLIVER:

Now, sir! what make you here?

ORLANDO:

Nothing; I am not taught to makeany thing.

OLIVER:

What mar you then, sir?

ORLANDO:

Marry, sir, I am helping you to mar that which God made, a poor unworthy brother of yours, with idleness.

OLIVER:

Marry, sir, be better employed, and benought awhile.

ORLANDO:

Shall I keep your hogs, and eat husks with them? What prodigal portion have I spent that I should come to such penury?

OLIVER:

Know you where you are, sir?

ORLANDO:

O, sir, very well; here in your orchard.

OLIVER:

Know you before whom, sir?

ORLANDO:

Ay, better than him I am before knows me. I know you are

my eldest brother; and in the gentle condition of blood, you should so know me. The courtesy of nations allows you my better in that you are the first-born; but the same tradition takes not away my blood, were there twenty brothers betwixt us. I have as much of my father in me as you, albeit I confess your coming before me is nearer to his reverence.

OLIVER:

What, boy!

[*Strikes him*]

ORLANDO:

Come, come, elder brother, you are too young in this.

OLIVER:

Wilt thou lay hands on me, villain?

ORLANDO:

I am no villain; I am the youngest son of Sir Rowland de Boys. He was my father; and he is thrice a villain that says such a father begot villains. Wert thou not my brother, I would not take this hand from thy throat till this other hadpull'd out thy tongue for saying so. Thou hasrail'd on thyself.

ADAM:

[Coming forward] Sweet masters, be patient; for your father's remembrance, be at accord.

OLIVER:

Let me go, I say.

ORLANDO:

I will not, till I please; you shall hear me. My father charg'd you in his will to give me good education: you have train'd me like a peasant, obscuring and hiding from me all gentleman-like qualities. The spirit of my father grows strong in me, and I will no longer endure it; therefore allow me such exercises as may become a gentleman, or give me the poor allottery my father left me by testament; with that I will go buy my fortunes.

OLIVER:

And what wilt thou do? Beg, when that is spent? Well, sir, get you in. I will not long be troubled with you; you shall have some part of your will. I pray you leave me.

ORLANDO:

I no further offend you than becomes me for my good.

OLIVER:

Get you with him, you old dog.

ADAM:

Is 'old dog' my reward? Most true, I have lost my teeth in

your service. God be with my old master! He would not have spoke such a word.

[Exeunt ORLANDO and ADAM

OLIVER:

Is it even so? Begin you to grow upon me? I will physic your rankness, and yet give no thousand crowns neither.

Holla, Dennis!

[*Enter DENNIS*]

DENNIS:

Calls your worship?

OLIVER:

not Charles, the Duke's wrestler, here to speak with me?

DENNIS:

So please you, he is here at the door and importunes access to you.

OLIVER:

Call him in. [*Exit DENNIS*] 'Twill be a good way; and tomorrow the wrestling is.

[*Enter CHARLES*]

CHARLES:

Good morrow to your worship.

OLIVER:

Good Monsieur Charles! What's the new news at the new court?

CHARLES:

There's no news at the court, sir, but the old news; that is, the old Duke is banished by his younger brother the new Duke; and three or four loving lords have put themselves into voluntary exile with him, whose lands and revenues enrich the new Duke; therefore he gives them good leave to wander.

OLIVER:

Can you tell if Rosalind, the Duke's daughter, be banished with her father?

CHARLES:

O, no; for the Duke's daughter, her cousin, so loves her, being ever from their cradles bred together, that she would have followed her exile, or have died to stay behind her. She is at the court, and no less beloved of her uncle than his own daughter; and never two ladies loved as they do.

OLIVER:

Where will the old Duke live?

CHARLES:

They say he is already in the Forest of Arden, and a many merry men with him; and there they live like the old Robin Hood of England. They say many young gentlemen flock to him every day, and fleet the time carelessly, as they did in the golden world.

OLIVER:

What, you wrestle to-morrow before the new Duke?

CHARLES:

Marry, do I, sir; and I came to acquaint you with a matter. I am given, sir, secretly to understand that your younger brother, Orlando, hath a disposition to come indisguis'd against me to try a fall. To-morrow, sir, I wrestle for my credit; and he that escapes me without some broken limb shall acquit him well.

Your brother is but young and tender; and, for your love, I would be loath to foil him, as I must, for my ownhonour, if he come in; therefore, out of my love to you, I came hither to acquaint you withal, that either you might stay him from his intendment, or brook such disgrace well as he shall run into, in that it is thing of his own search and altogether against my will.

OLIVER:

Charles, I thank thee for thy love to me, which thoushalt find

I will most kindly requite. I had myself notice of my brother's purpose herein, and have by underhand means laboured to dissuade him from it; but he is resolute. I'll tell thee, Charles, it is the stubbornest young fellow of France; full of ambition, an envious emulator of every man's good parts, a secret and villainous contriver against me his natural brother. Therefore use thy discretion: I had aslief thou didst break his neck as his finger. And thou wert best look to't; for if thou dost him any slight disgrace, or if he do not mightily grace himself on thee, he will practise against thee by poison, entrap thee by some treacherous device, and never leave thee till he hath ta'en thy life by some indirect means or other; for, I assure thee, and almost with tears I speak it, there is not one so young and so villainous this day living. I speak but brotherly of him; but should I anatomize him to thee as he is, I must blush and weep, and thou must look pale and wonder.

CHARLES:

I am heartily glad I came hither to you. If he come to-morrow I'll give him his payment. If ever he go alone again, I'll never wrestle for prize more. And so, God keep your worship!

[*Exit*]

OLIVER:

Farewell, good Charles. Now will I stir this gamester. I hope I shall see an end of him; for my soul, yet I know not why, hates nothing more than he. Yet he's gentle; neverschool'd and yet learned; full of noble device; of all sorts enchantingly beloved; and, indeed, so much in the heart of the world, and especially of my own people, who best know him, that I am altogethermisprised. But it shall not be so long; this wrestler shall clear all. Nothing remains but that I kindle the boy thither, which now I'll go about.

[*Exit*]

SCENE II.
A lawn before the DUKE'S palace

[*Enter ROSALIND and CELIA*]

CELIA:

I pray thee, Rosalind, sweet my coz, be merry.

ROSALIND:

Dear Celia, I show more mirth than I am mistress of; and would you yet I were merrier? Unless you could teach me to forget a banished father, you must not learn me how to remember any extraordinary pleasure.

CELIA:

Herein I see thoulov'st me not with the full weight that I love thee. If my uncle, thy banished father, had banished thy uncle, the Duke my father, so thouhadst been still with me, I could have taught my love to take thy father for mine; so wouldst thou, if the truth of thy love to me were so righteouslytemper'd as mine is to thee.

ROSALIND:

Well, I will forget the condition of my estate, to rejoice in yours.

CELIA:

You know my father hath no child but I, nor none is like to have; and, truly, when he dies thoushalt be his heir; for what he hath taken away from thy father perforce, I will render thee again in affection. By minehonour, I will; and when I break that oath, let me turn monster; therefore, my sweet Rose, my dear Rose, be merry.

ROSALIND:

From henceforth I will, coz, and devise sports.

Let me see; what think you of falling in love?

CELIA:

Marry, Iprithee, do, to make sport withal; but love no man in good earnest, nor no further in sport neither than with safety of a pure blush thoumayst in honour come off again.

ROSALIND:

What shall be our sport, then?

CELIA:

Let us sit and mock the good housewife Fortune from her wheel, that her gifts may henceforth be bestowed equally.

ROSALIND:

I would we could do so; for her benefits are mightily misplaced; and the bountiful blind woman doth most mistake in her gifts to women.

CELIA:

'Tis true; for those that she makes fair she scarce makes honest; and those that she makes honest she makes very ill-favouredly.

ROSALIND:

Nay; now thougoest from Fortune's office to Nature's:
Fortune reigns in gifts of the world, not in the lineaments of Nature.

[*Enter TOUCHSTONE*]

CELIA:

No; when Nature hath made a fair creature, may she not by Fortune fall into the fire? Though Nature hath given us wit to flout at Fortune, hath not Fortune sent in this fool to cut off the argument?

ROSALIND:

Indeed, there is Fortune too hard for Nature, when Fortune makes Nature's natural the cutter-off of Nature's wit.

CELIA:

Peradventure this is not Fortune's work neither, but Nature's, whoperceiveth our natural wits too dull to reason of such goddesses, and hath sent this natural for our whetstone; for always the dullness of the fool is the whetstone of the wits.

How now, wit! Whither wander you?

TOUCHSTONE:

Mistress, you must come away to your father.

CELIA:

Were you made the messenger?

TOUCHSTONE:

No, by minehonour; but I was bid to come for you.

ROSALIND:

Where learned you that oath, fool?

TOUCHSTONE:

Of a certain knight that swore by hishonour they were good pancakes, and swore by hishonour the mustard was naught. Now I'll stand to it, the pancakes were naught and the mustard was good, and yet was not the knight forsworn.

CELIA:

How prove you that, in the great heap of your knowledge?

ROSALIND:

Ay, marry, nowunmuzzle your wisdom.

TOUCHSTONE:

Stand you both forth now: stroke your chins, and swear by your beards that I am a knave.

CELIA:

By our beards, if we had them, thou art.

TOUCHSTONE:

By my knavery, if I had it, then I were. But if you swear by that that not, you are not forsworn; no more was this knight, swearing by hishonour, for he never had any; or if he had, he had sworn it away before ever he saw thosepancackes or that mustard.

CELIA:

Prithee, who is't that thou mean'st?

TOUCHSTONE:

One that old Frederick, your father, loves.

CELIA:

My father's love is enough tohonour him. Enough, speak no more of him; you'll bewhipt for taxation one of these days.

TOUCHSTONE:

The more pity that fools may not speak wisely what wise men do foolishly.

CELIA:

By my troth, thousayest true; for since the little wit that fools have was silenced, the little foolery that wise men have makes a great show. Here comes Monsieur Le Beau.

[*Enter LE BEAU*]

ROSALIND:

With his mouth full of news.

CELIA:

Which he will put on us as pigeons feed their young.

ROSALIND:

Then shall we be news-cramm'd.

CELIA:

All the better; we shall be the more marketable. Bon jour,

Monsieur Le Beau. What's the news?

LE BEAU:

Fair Princess, you have lost much good sport.

CELIA:

Sport! of whatcolour?

LE BEAU:

What colour, madam? How shall I answer you?

ROSALIND:

As wit and fortune will.

TOUCHSTONE:

Or as the Destinies decrees.

CELIA:

Well said; that was laid on with a trowel.

TOUCHSTONE:

Nay, if I keep not my rank-

ROSALIND:

Thoulosest thy old smell.

LE BEAU:

You amaze me, ladies. I would have told you of good wrestling, which you have lost the sight of.

ROSALIND:

Yet tell us the manner of the wrestling.

LE BEAU:

I will tell you the beginning, and, if it please your ladyships, you may see the end; for the best is yet to do; and here, where you are, they are coming to perform it.

CELIA:

Well, the beginning, that is dead and buried.

LE BEAU:

There comes an old man and his three sons-

CELIA:

I could match this beginning with an old tale.

LE BEAU:

Three proper young men, of excellent growth and presence.

ROSALIND:

With bills on their necks: 'Be it known unto all men by these presents'-

LE BEAU:

The eldest of the three wrestled with Charles, the Duke's wrestler; which Charles in a moment threw him, and broke three of his ribs, that there is little hope of life in him. So heserv'd the second, and so the third. Yonder they lie; the poor old man, their father, making such pitiful dole over them that all the beholders take his part with weeping.

ROSALIND:

Alas!

TOUCHSTONE:

But what is the sport, monsieur, that the ladies have lost?

LE BEAU:

Why, this that I speak of.

TOUCHSTONE:

Thus men may grow wiser every day. It is the first time that ever I heard breaking of ribs was sport for ladies.

CELIA:

Or I, I promise thee.

ROSALIND:

But is there any else longs to see this broken music in his sides? Is there yet another dotes upon rib-breaking?

Shall we see this wrestling, cousin?

LE BEAU:

You must, if you stay here; for here is the place appointed for the wrestling, and they are ready to perform it.

CELIA:

Yonder, sure, they are coming. Let us now stay and see it.

[*Flourish. Enter DUKE FREDERICK, LORDS, ORLANDO, CHARLES, and ATTENDANTS*]

FREDERICK:

Come on; since the youth will not be entreated, his own peril on his forwardness.

ROSALIND:

Is yonder the man?

LE BEAU:

Even he, madam.

CELIA:

Alas, he is too young; yet he looks successfully.

FREDERICK:

How now, daughter and cousin! Are you crept hither to see the wrestling?

ROSALIND:

Ay, my liege; so please you give us leave.

FREDERICK:

You will take little delight in it, I can tell you, there is such odds in the man. In pity of the challenger's youth I would fain dissuade him, but he will not be entreated.

Speak to him, ladies; see if you can move him.

CELIA:

Call him hither, good Monsieur Le Beau.

FREDERICK:

Do so; I'll not be by.

[*DUKE FREDERICK goes apart*]

LE BEAU:

Monsieur the Challenger, the Princess calls for you.

ORLANDO:

I attend them with all respect and duty.

ROSALIND:

Young man, have you challeng'd Charles the wrestler?

ORLANDO:

No, fair Princess; he is the general challenger. I come but in, as others do, to try with him the strength of my youth.

CELIA:

Young gentleman, your spirits are too bold for your years. You have seen cruel proof of this man's strength; if you saw yourself with your eyes, or knew yourself with your judgment, the fear of your adventure would counsel you to a more equal enterprise. We pray you, for your own sake, to embrace your own safety and give over this attempt.

ROSALIND:

Do, young sir; your reputation shall not therefore be misprised: we will make it our suit to the Duke that the wrestling might not go forward.

ORLANDO:

I beseech you, punish me not with your hard thoughts, wherein I confess me much guilty to deny so fair and excellent ladiesany thing. But let your fair eyes and gentle wishes go with me to my trial; wherein if I befoil'd there is but one sham'd that was never gracious; if kill'd, but one dead that is willing to be so. I shall do my friends no wrong, for I have none to lament me; the world no injury, for in it I have nothing; only in the world I fill up a place, which may be better supplied when I have made it empty.

ROSALIND:

The little strength that I have, I would it were with you.

CELIA:

And mine to eke out hers.

ROSALIND:

Fare you well. Pray heaven I bedeceiv'd in you!

CELIA:

Your heart's desires be with you!

CHARLES:

Come, where is this young gallant that is so desirous to lie with his mother earth?

ORLANDO:

Ready, sir; but his will hath in it a more modest working.

FREDERICK:

You shall try but one fall.

CHARLES:

No, I warrant your Grace, you shall not entreat him to a second, that have so mightily persuaded him from a first.

ORLANDO:

You mean to mock me after; you should not havemock'd me before; but come your ways.

ROSALIND:

Now, Hercules be thy speed, young man!

CELIA:

I would I were invisible, to catch the strong fellow by the leg.

[*They wrestle*]

ROSALIND:

O excellent young man!

CELIA:

If I had a thunderbolt in mine eye, I can tell who should down.

[*CHARLES is thrown. Shout*]

FREDERICK:

No more, no more.

ORLANDO:

Yes, I beseech your Grace; I am not yet wellbreath'd.

FREDERICK:

How dost thou, Charles?

LE BEAU:

He cannot speak, my lord.

FREDERICK:

Bear him away. What is thy name, young man?

ORLANDO:

Orlando, my liege; the youngest son of Sir Rowland de Boys.

FREDERICK:

I would thouhadst been son to some man else.

The worldesteem'd thy father honourable,

But I did find him still mine enemy.

Thoushouldst have better pleas'd me with this deed,

Hadst thou descended from another house.

But fare thee well; thou art a gallant youth;

I would thouhadst told me of another father.

[*Exeunt DUKE, train, and LE BEAU*]

CELIA:

Were I my father, coz, would I do this?

ORLANDO:

I am more proud to be Sir Rowland's son,

His youngest son- and would not change that calling

To be adopted heir to Frederick.

ROSALIND:

My fatherlov'd Sir Rowland as his soul,

And all the world was of my father's mind;

Had I before known this young man his son,

I should have given him tears unto entreaties

Ere he should thus haveventur'd.

CELIA:

Gentle cousin,

Let us go thank him, and encourage him;

My father's rough and envious disposition

Sticks me at heart. Sir, you have welldeserv'd;

If you do keep your promises in love

But justly as you have exceeded all promise,

Your mistress shall be happy.

ROSALIND:

Gentleman,

[*Giving him a chain from her neck*]

Wear this for me; one out of suits with fortune,

That could give more, but that her hand lacks means.

Shall we go, coz?

CELIA:

Ay. Fare you well, fair gentleman.

ORLANDO:

Can I not say 'I thank you'? My better parts

Are all thrown down; and that which here stands up

Is but aquintain, a mere lifeless block.

ROSALIND:

He calls us back. My pride fell with my fortunes;

I'll ask him what he would. Did you call, sir?

Sir, you have wrestled well, and overthrown

More than your enemies.

CELIA:

Will you go, coz?

ROSALIND:

Have with you. Fare you well.

[*Exeunt ROSALIND and CELIA*]

ORLANDO:

What passion hangs these weights upon my tongue?

I cannot speak to her, yet sheurg'd conference.

O poor Orlando, thou art overthrown!

Or Charles or something weaker masters thee.

[*Re-enter LE BEAU*]

LE BEAU:

Good sir, I do in friendship counsel you
To leave this place. Albeit you havedeserv'd
High commendation, true applause, and love,
Yet such is now the Duke's condition
That he misconstrues all that you have done.
The Duke is humorous; what he is, indeed,
More suits you to conceive than I to speak of.

ORLANDO:

I thank you, sir; and pray you tell me this:
Which of the two was daughter of the Duke
That here was at the wrestling?

LE BEAU:

Neither his daughter, if we judge by manners;
But yet, indeed, the smaller is his daughter;
The other is daughter to thebanish'd Duke,
And heredetain'd by her usurping uncle,

To keep his daughter company; whose loves
Are dearer than the natural bond of sisters.
But I can tell you that of late this Duke
Hath ta'en displeasure 'gainst his gentle niece,
Grounded upon no other argument
But that the people praise her for her virtues
And pity her for her good father's sake;
And, on my life, his malice 'gainst the lady
Will suddenly break forth. Sir, fare you well.
Hereafter, in a better world than this,
I shall desire more love and knowledge of you.

ORLANDO:

I rest much bounden to you; fare you well.

[*Exit LE BEAU*]

Thus must I from the smoke into the smother;
From tyrant Duke unto a tyrant brother.
But heavenly Rosalind!

[*Exit*]

SCENE III.
The DUKE's palace

[*Enter CELIA and ROSALIND*]

CELIA:

Why, cousin! why, Rosalind! Cupid have mercy! Not a word?

ROSALIND:

Not one to throw at a dog.

CELIA:

No, thy words are too precious to be cast away upon curs; throw some of them at me; come, lame me with reasons.

ROSALIND:

Then there were two cousins laid up, when the one should belam'd with reasons and the other mad without any.

CELIA:

But is all this for your father?

ROSALIND:

No, some of it is for my child's father. O, how full of briers is this working-day world!

CELIA:

They are but burs, cousin, thrown upon thee in holiday foolery; if we walk not in the trodden paths, our very petticoats will catch them.

ROSALIND:

I could shake them off my coat: these burs are in my heart.

CELIA:

Hem them away.

ROSALIND:

I would try, if I could cry 'hem' and have him.

CELIA:

Come, come, wrestle with thy affections.

ROSALIND:

O, they take the part of a better wrestler than myself.

CELIA:

O, a good wish upon you! You will try in time, in despite of a fall. But, turning these jests out of service, let us talk in good earnest. Is it possible, on such a sudden, you should fall into so strong a liking with old Sir Rowland's youngest son?

ROSALIND:

The Duke my fatherlov'd his father dearly.

CELIA:

Doth it therefore ensue that you should love his son dearly?
By this kind of chase I should hate him, for my father hated
his father dearly; yet I hate not Orlando.

ROSALIND:

No, faith, hate him not, for my sake.

CELIA:

Why should I not? Doth he not deserve well?

[*Enter DUKE FREDERICK, with LORDS*]

ROSALIND:

Let me love him for that; and do you love him because I do.
Look, here comes the Duke.

CELIA:

With his eyes full of anger.

FREDERICK:

Mistress, dispatch you with your safest haste,

And get you from our court.

ROSALIND:

Me, uncle?

FREDERICK:

You, cousin.

Within these ten days if that thoubeest found

So near our public court as twenty miles,

Thoudiest for it.

ROSALIND:

I do beseech your Grace,

Let me the knowledge of my fault bear with me.

If with myself I hold intelligence,

Or have acquaintance with mine own desires;

If that I do not dream, or be not frantic-

As I do trust I am not- then, dear uncle,

Never so much as in a thought unborn

Did I offend your Highness.

FREDERICK:

Thus do all traitors;

If their purgation did consist in words,

They are as innocent as grace itself.

Let it suffice thee that I trust thee not.

ROSALIND:

Yet your mistrust cannot make me a traitor.

Tell mewhereon the likelihood depends.

FREDERICK:

Thou art thy father's daughter; there's enough.

ROSALIND:

SO was I when your Highness took his dukedom;

So was I when your Highness banish'd him.
Treason is not inherited, my lord;
Or, if we did derive it from our friends,
What's that to me? My father was no traitor.
Then, good my liege, mistake me not so much
To think my poverty is treacherous.

CELIA:

Dear sovereign, hear me speak.

FREDERICK:

Ay, Celia; we stay'd her for your sake,
Else had she with her father rang'd along.

CELIA:

I did not then entreat to have her stay;
It was your pleasure, and your own remorse;
I was too young that time to value her,
But now I know her. If she be a traitor,
Why so am I: we still have slept together,
Rose at an instant, learn'd, play'd, eat together;
And wheresoe'er we went, like Juno's swans,
Still we went coupled and inseparable.

FREDERICK:

She is too subtle for thee; and her smoothness,
Her very silence and her patience,

Speak to the people, and they pity her.

Thou art a fool. She robs thee of thy name;

And thou wilt show more bright and seem more virtuous

When she is gone. Then open not thy lips.

Firm and irrevocable is my doom

Which I havepass'd upon her; she is banish'd.

CELIA:

Pronounce that sentence, then, on me, my liege;

I cannot live out of her company.

FREDERICK:

You are a fool. You, niece, provide yourself.

If you outstay the time, upon minehonour,

And in the greatness of my word, you die.

[*Exeunt DUKE and LORDS*]

CELIA:

O my poor Rosalind! Whither wilt thou go?

Wilt thou change fathers? I will givethee mine.

I charge thee be not thou moregriev'd than I am.

ROSALIND:

I have more cause.

CELIA:

Thou hast not, cousin.

Prithee be cheerful. Know'st thou not the Duke
Hath banish'd me, his daughter?

ROSALIND:

That he hath not.

CELIA:

No, hath not? Rosalind lacks, then, the love
Which teacheth thee that thou and I am one.
Shall we be sund'red? Shall we part, sweet girl?
No; let my father seek another heir.
Therefore devise with me how we may fly,
Whither to go, and what to bear with us;
And do not seek to take your charge upon you,
To bear your griefs yourself, and leave me out;
For, by this heaven, now at our sorrows pale,
Say what thou canst, I'll go along with thee.

ROSALIND:

Why, whither shall we go?

CELIA:

To seek my uncle in the Forest of Arden.

ROSALIND:

Alas, what danger will it be to us,
Maids as we are, to travel forth so far!

Beautyprovoketh thieves sooner than gold.

CELIA:

I'll put myself in poor and mean attire,
And with a kind of umber smirch my face;
Thelike do you; so shall we pass along,
And never stir assailants.

ROSALIND:

Were it not better,
Because that I am more than common tall,
That I did suit me all points like a man?
A gallantcurtle-axe upon my thigh,
A boar spear in my hand; and- in my heart
Lie there what hidden woman's fear there will-
We'll have a swashing and a martial outside,
As many other mannish cowards have
That do outface it with their semblances.

CELIA:

What shall I call thee when thou art a man?

ROSALIND:

I'll have no worse a name than Jove's own page,
And therefore look you call me Ganymede.
But what will you becall'd?

CELIA:

Something that hath a reference to my state:
No longer Celia, but Aliena.

ROSALIND:

But, cousin, what if we assay'd to steal
The clownish fool out of your father's court?
Would he not be a comfort to our travel?

CELIA:

He'll go along o'er the wide world with me;
Leave me alone to woo him. Let's away,
And get our jewels and our wealth together;
Devise the fittest time and safest way
To hide us from pursuit that will be made
After my flight. Now go we in content
To liberty, and not to banishment.

[*Exeunt*]

ACT 2.

SCENE I.
The Forest of Arden

[*Enter DUKE SENIOR, AMIENS, and two or three LORDS, like foresters*]

DUKE SENIOR:
  Now, my co-mates and brothers in exile,
  Hath not old custom made this life more sweet
  Than that of painted pomp? Are not these woods
  More free from peril than the envious court?
  Here feel we not the penalty of Adam,
  The seasons' difference; as the icy fang
  And churlish chiding of the winter's wind,

Which when it bites and blows upon my body,
Even till I shrink with cold, I smile and say
'This is no flattery; these arecounsellors
That feelingly persuade me what I am.'
Sweet are the uses of adversity,
Which, like the toad, ugly and venomous,
Wears yet a precious jewel in his head;
And this our life, exempt from public haunt,
Finds tongues in trees, books in the running brooks,
Sermons in stones, and good in everything.
I would not change it.

AMIENS:

Happy is your Grace,
That can translate the stubbornness of fortune
Into so quiet and so sweet a style.

DUKE SENIOR:

Come, shall we go and kill us venison?
And yet it irks me the poor dappled fools,
Being native burghers of this desert city,
Should, in their own confines, with forked heads
Have their round haunchesgor'd.

FIRST LORD:

Indeed, my lord,

The melancholy Jaques grieves at that;
And, in that kind, swears you do more usurp
Than doth your brother that hath banish'd you.
To-day my Lord of Amiens and myself
Did steal behind him as he lay along
Under an oak whose antique root peeps out
Upon the brook that brawls along this wood!
To the which place a poor sequest'red stag,
That from the hunter's aim had ta'en a hurt,
Did come to languish; and, indeed, my lord,
The wretched animal heav'd forth such groans
That their discharge did stretch his leathern coat
Almost to bursting; and the big round tears
Cours'd one another down his innocent nose
In piteous chase; and thus the hairy fool,
Much marked of the melancholy Jaques,
Stood on th' extremest verge of the swift brook,
Augmenting it with tears.

DUKE SENIOR:

But what said Jaques?
Did he not moralize this spectacle?

FIRST LORD:

O, yes, into a thousand similes.

First, for his weeping into the needless stream:
'Poor deer,' quoth he 'thou mak'st a testament
As worldlings do, giving thy sum of more
To that which had too much.' Then, being there alone,
Left and abandoned of his velvet friends:
' 'Tis right'; quoth he 'thus misery doth part
The flux of company.' Anon, a careless herd,
Full of the pasture, jumps along by him
And never stays to greet him. 'Ay,' quoth Jaques
'Sweep on, you fat and greasy citizens;
'Tis just the fashion. Wherefore do you look
Upon that poor and broken bankrupt there?'
Thus most invectively he pierceth through
The body of the country, city, court,
Yea, and of this our life; swearing that we
Are mere usurpers, tyrants, and what's worse,
To fright the animals, and to kill them up
In their assign'd and native dwelling-place.

DUKE SENIOR:

And did you leave him in this contemplation?

SECOND LORD:

We did, my lord, weeping and commenting
Upon the sobbing deer.

DUKE SENIOR:

Show me the place;

I love to cope him in these sullen fits,

For then he's full of matter.

FIRST LORD:

I'll bring you to him straight.

[*Exeunt*]

SCENE II.
The DUKE'S palace

[*Enter DUKE FREDERICK, with LORDS*]

FREDERICK:

Can it be possible that no man saw them?

It cannot be; some villains of my court

Are of consent and sufferance in this.

FIRST LORD:

I cannot hear of any that did see her.

The ladies, her attendants of her chamber,

Saw her abed, and in the morning early
They found the bed untreasur'd of their mistress.

SECOND LORD:

My lord, the roynish clown, at whom so oft
Your Grace was wont to laugh, is also missing.
Hisperia, the Princess' gentlewoman,
Confesses that she secretly o'erheard
Your daughter and her cousin much commend
The parts and graces of the wrestler
That did but lately foil the sinewy Charles;
And she believes, wherever they are gone,
That youth is surely in their company.

FREDERICK:

Send to his brother; fetch that gallant hither.
If he be absent, bring his brother to me;
I'll make him find him. Do this suddenly;
And let not search and inquisition quail
To bring again these foolish runaways.

[*Exeunt*]

SCENE III.
Before OLIVER'S house

[*Enter ORLANDO and ADAM, meeting*]

ORLANDO:
 Who's there?
ADAM:
 What, my young master? O my gentle master!
 O my sweet master! O you memory
 Of old Sir Rowland! Why, what make you here?
 Why are you virtuous? Why do people love you?
 And wherefore are you gentle, strong, and valiant?
 Why would you be so fond to overcome
 The bonnyprizer of the humorous Duke?
 Your praise is come too swiftly home before you.
 Know you not, master, to some kind of men
 Their graces serve them but as enemies?
 No more do yours. Your virtues, gentle master,
 Are sanctified and holy traitors to you.
 O, what a world is this, when what is comely

Envenoms him that bears it!

ORLANDO:

Why, what's the matter?

ADAM:

O unhappy youth!

Come not within these doors; within this roof

The enemy of all your graces lives.

Your brother- no, no brother; yet the son-

Yet not the son; I will not call him son

Of him I was about to call his father-

Hath heard your praises; and this night he means

To burn the lodging where you use to lie,

And you within it. If he fail of that,

He will have other means to cut you off;

I overheard him and his practices.

This is no place; this house is but a butchery;

Abhor it, fear it, do not enter it.

ORLANDO:

Why, whither, Adam, wouldst thou have me go?

ADAM:

No matter whither, so you come not here.

ORLANDO:

What, wouldst thou have me go and beg my food,

Or with a base andboist'rous sword enforce
A thievish living on the common road?
This I must do, or know not what to do;
Yet this I will not do, do how I can.
I rather will subject me to the malice
Of a diverted blood and bloody brother.

ADAM:

But do not so. I have five hundred crowns,
The thrifty hire Isav'd under your father,
Which I did store to be my foster-nurse,
When service should in my old limbs lie lame,
Andunregarded age in corners thrown.
Take that, and He that doth the ravens feed,
Yea, providently caters for the sparrow,
Be comfort to my age! Here is the gold;
All this I give you. Let me be your servant;
Though I look old, yet I am strong and lusty;
For in my youth I never did apply
Hot and rebellious liquors in my blood,
Nor did not withunbashful forehead woo
The means of weakness and debility;
Therefore my age is as a lusty winter,
Frosty, but kindly. Let me go with you;

I'll do the service of a younger man
In all your business and necessities.

ORLANDO:

O good old man, how well in thee appears
The constant service of the antique world,
When service sweat for duty, not formeed!
Thou art not for the fashion of these times,
Where none will sweat but for promotion,
And having that do choke their service up
Even with the having; it is not so with thee.
But, poor old man, thouprun'st a rotten tree
That cannot so much as a blossom yield
In lieu of all thy pains and husbandry.
But come thy ways, we'll go along together,
Andere we have thy youthful wages spent
We'll light upon some settled low content.

ADAM:

Master, go on; and I will follow the
To the last gasp, with truth and loyalty.
From seventeen years till now almost four-score
Here lived I, but now live here no more.
At seventeen years many their fortunes seek,
But at fourscore it is too late a week;

Yet fortune cannot recompense me better

Than to die well and not my master's debtor.

[*Exeunt*]

SCENE IV.
The Forest of Arden

[*Enter ROSALIND for GANYMEDE, CELIA for ALIENA, and CLOWN alias TOUCHSTONE*]

ROSALIND:

O Jupiter, how weary are my spirits!

TOUCHSTONE:

I Care not for my spirits, if my legs were not weary.

ROSALIND:

I could find in my heart to disgrace my man's apparel, and to cry like a woman; but I must comfort the weaker vessel, as doublet and hose ought to show itself courageous to petticoat; therefore, courage, goodAliena.

CELIA:

I pray you bear with me; I cannot go no further.

TOUCHSTONE:

For my part, I had rather bear with you than bear you; yet I should bear no cross if I did bear you; for I think you have no money in your purse.

ROSALIND:

Well,. this is the Forest of Arden.

TOUCHSTONE:

Ay, now am I in Arden; the more fool I; when I was at home I was in a better place; buttravellers must be content.

[*Enter CORIN and SILVIUS*]

ROSALIND:

Ay, be so, good Touchstone. Look you, who comes here, a young man and an old in solemn talk.

CORIN:

That is the way to make her scorn you still.

SILVIUS:

O Corin, that thou knew'st how I do love her!

CORIN:

I partly guess; for I havelov'd ere now.

SILVIUS:

No, Corin, being old, thou canst not guess,
Though in thy youth thouwast as true a lover
As eversigh'd upon a midnight pillow.
But ifthy love were ever like to mine,
As sure I think did never man love so,
How many actions most ridiculous
Hast thou been drawn to by thy fantasy?

CORIN:

Into a thousand that I have forgotten.

SILVIUS:

O, thou didst then never love so heartily!
If thourememb'rest not the slightest folly
That ever love did make thee run into,
Thou hast notlov'd;
Or if thou hast not sat as I do now,
Wearing thy hearer in thy mistress' praise,
Thou hast notlov'd;
Or if thou hast not broke from company
Abruptly, as my passion now makes me,
Thou hast notlov'd.
OPhebe, Phebe, Phebe!

[*Exit Silvius*]

ROSALIND:

Alas, poor shepherd! searching of thy wound, I have by hard adventure found mine own.

TOUCHSTONE:

And I mine. I remember, when I was in love, I broke my sword upon a stone, and bid him take that for coming a-night to Jane Smile; and I remember the kissing of herbatler, and the cow's dugs that her prettychopt hands had milk'd; and I remember the wooing ofpeascod instead of her; from whom I took two cods, and giving her them again, said with weeping tears 'Wear these for my sake.' We that are true lovers run into strange capers; but as all is mortal in nature, so is all nature in love mortal in folly.

ROSALIND:

Thouspeak'st wiser than thou art ware of.

TOUCHSTONE:

Nay, I shall ne'erbe ware of mine own wit till I break my shins against it.

ROSALIND:

Jove, Jove! this shepherd's passion Is much upon my fashion.

TOUCHSTONE:

And mine; but it grows something stale with me.

CELIA:

I pray you, one of you question yond man

If he for gold will give us any food;

I faint almost to death.

TOUCHSTONE:

Holla, you clown!

ROSALIND:

Peace, fool; he's not thyEnsman.

CORIN:

Who calls?

TOUCHSTONE:

Your betters, sir.

CORIN:

Else are they very wretched.

ROSALIND:

Peace, I say. Good even to you, friend.

CORIN:

And to you, gentle sir, and to you all.

ROSALIND:

Iprithee, shepherd, if that love or gold

Can in this desert place buy entertainment,

Bring us where we may rest ourselves and feed.

Here's a young maid with travel muchoppress'd,
And faints forsuccour.

CORIN:

Fair sir, I pity her,
And wish, for her sake more than for mine own,
My fortunes were more able to relieve her;
But I am shepherd to another man,
And do not shear the fleeces that I graze.
My master is of churlish disposition,
And littlerecks to find the way to heaven
By doing deeds of hospitality.
Besides, his cote, his flocks, and bounds of feed,
Are now on sale; and at our sheepcote now,
By reason of his absence, there is nothing
That you will feed on; but what is, come see,
And in my voice most welcome shall you be.

ROSALIND:

What is he that shall buy his flock and pasture?

CORIN:

That young swain that you saw here but erewhile,
That little cares for buyingany thing.

ROSALIND:

I pray thee, if it stand with honesty,

Buy thou the cottage, pasture, and the flock,

And thoushalt have to pay for it of us.

CELIA:

And we will mend thy wages. I like this place,

And willingly could waste my time in it.

CORIN:

Assuredly the thing is to be sold.

Go with me; if you like upon report

The soil, the profit, and this kind of life,

I will your very faithful feeder be,

And buy it with your gold right suddenly.

[*Exeunt*]

SCENE V.
Another part of the forest

[*Enter AMIENS, JAQUES, and OTHERS*]

[*SONG*]

AMIENS:

> Under the greenwood tree
>
> Who loves to lie with me,
>
> And turn his merry note
>
> Unto the sweet bird's throat,
>
> Come hither, come hither, come hither.
>
> Here shall he see
>
> No enemy
>
> But winter and rough weather.

JAQUES:

More, more, Iprithee, more.

AMIENS:

It will make you melancholy, MonsieurJaques.

JAQUES:

I thank it. More, Iprithee, more. I can suck melancholy out of a song, as a weasel sucks eggs. More, Iprithee, more.

AMIENS:

My voice is ragged; I know I cannot please you.

JAQUES:

I do not desire you to please me; I do desire you to sing. Come, more; anotherstanzo. Call you 'em stanzos?

AMIENS:

What you will, MonsieurJaques.

JAQUES:

Nay, I care not for their names; they owe me nothing. Will you sing?

AMIENS:

More at your request than to please myself.

JAQUES:

Well then, if ever I thank any man, I'll thank you; but that they call compliment is liketh' encounter of two dog-apes; and when a man thanks me heartily, methinks have given him a penny, and he renders me the beggarly thanks. Come, sing; and you that will not, hold your tongues.

AMIENS:

Well, I'll end the song. Sirs, cover the while; the Duke will drink under this tree. He hath been all this day to look you.

JAQUES:

And I have been all this day to avoid him. He is to disputable for my company. I think of as many matters as he; but I give heaven thanks, and make no boast of them. Come, warble, come.

[*SONG*]

[*All together here*]

Who doth ambition shun,

And loves to livei' th' sun,

Seeking the food he eats,

Andpleas'd with what he gets,

Come hither, come hither, come hither.

Here shall he see

No enemy

But winter and rough weather.

JAQUES:

I'll give you a verse to this note that I made yesterday in despite of my invention.

AMIENS:

And I'll sing it.

JAQUES:

Thus it goes:

If it do come to pass

That any man turn ass,

Leaving his wealth and ease

A stubborn will to please,

Ducdame, ducdame, ducdame;

Here shall he see

Gross fools as he,

An if he will come to me.

AMIENS:

What's that 'ducdame'?

JAQUES:

'Tis a Greek invocation, to call fools into a circle. I'll go sleep, if I can; if I cannot, I'll rail against all the first-born of Egypt.

AMIENS:

And I'll go seek the Duke; his banquet isprepar'd.

[*Exeunt severally*]

SCENE VI.
The forest

[*Enter ORLANDO and ADAM*]

ADAM:

Dear master, I can go no further. O, I die for food! Here lie I down, and measure out my grave. Farewell, kind master.

ORLANDO:

Why, how now, Adam! No greater heart in thee? Live a little; comfort a little; cheer thyself a little. If this uncouth forest yield anything savage, I will either be food for it or bring it for food to thee. Thy conceit is nearer death than thy powers. For my sake be comfortable; hold death awhile at the arm's end. I will here be with the presently; and if I bring thee not something to eat, I will give thee leave to die; but if thou diest before I come, thou art a mocker of my labour. Well said! thoulook'st cheerly; and I'll be with thee quickly. Yet thou liest in the bleak air. Come, I will bear thee to some shelter; and thoushalt not die for lack of a dinner, if there live anything in this desert. Cheerly, good Adam!

[*Exeunt*]

SCENE VII.
The forest

[*A table set out. Enter DUKE SENIOR, AMIENS, and LORDS, like outlaws*]

DUKE SENIOR:

    I think he betransform'd into a beast;

    For I can nowhere find him like a man.

FIRST LORD:

    My lord, he is but even now gone hence;

    Here was he merry, hearing of a song.

DUKE SENIOR:

    If he, compact of jars, grow musical,

    We shall have shortly discord in the spheres.

    Go seek him; tell him I would speak with him.

[*Enter JAQUES*]

FIRST LORD:

    He saves mylabour by his own approach.

DUKE SENIOR:

    Why, how now, monsieur! what a life is this,

    That your poor friends must woo your company?

    What, you look merrily!

JAQUES:

    A fool, a fool! I met a fooli' th' forest,

    A motley fool. A miserable world!

    As I do live by food, I met a fool,

Who laid him down andbask'd him in the sun,

Andrail'd on Lady Fortune in good terms,

In good set terms- and yet a motley fool.

'Good morrow, fool,'quoth I; 'No, sir,' quoth he,

'Call me not fool till heaven hath sent me fortune.'

And then he drew a dial from his poke,

And, looking on it with lack-lustre eye,

Says very wisely, 'It is ten o'clock;

Thus we may see,'quoth he, 'how the world wags;

'Tis but an hour ago since it was nine;

And after one hour more 'twill be eleven;

And so, from hour to hour, we ripe and ripe,

And then, from hour to hour, we rot and rot;

And thereby hangs a tale.' When I did hear

The motley fool thus moral on the time,

My lungs began to crow like chanticleer

That fools should be so deep contemplative;

And I did laugh sans intermission

An hour by his dial. O noble fool!

A worthy fool! Motley's the only wear.

DUKE SENIOR:

What fool is this?

JAQUES:

O worthy fool! One that hath been a courtier,
And says, if ladies be but young and fair,
They have the gift to know it; and in his brain,
Which is as dry as the remainder biscuit
After a voyage, he hath strange placescramm'd
With observation, the which he vents
In mangled forms. O that I were a fool!
I am ambitious for a motley coat.

DUKE SENIOR:

Thoushalt have one.

JAQUES:

It is my only suit,
Provided that you weed your better judgments
Of all opinion that grows rank in them
That I am wise. I must have liberty
Withal, as large a charter as the wind,
To blow on whom I please, for so fools have;
And they that are most galled with my folly,
They most must laugh. And why, sir, must they so?
The why is plain as way to parish church:
He that a fool doth very wisely hit
Doth very foolishly, although he smart,
Not to seem senseless of the bob; if not,

The wise man's folly isanatomiz'd
Even by thesquand'ring glances of the fool.
Invest me in my motley; give me leave
To speak my mind, and I will through and through
Cleanse the foul body ofth' infected world,
If they will patiently receive my medicine.

DUKE SENIOR:

Fie on thee! I can tell what thou wouldst do.

JAQUES:

What, for a counter, would I do but good?

DUKE SENIOR:

Most Mischievous foul sin, in chiding sin;
For thou thyself hast been a libertine,
As sensual as the brutish sting itself;
And allth' embossed sores and headed evils
That thou with license of free foot hast caught
Wouldst thou disgorge into the general world.

JAQUES:

Why, who cries out on pride
That can therein tax any private party?
Doth it not flow as hugely as the sea,
Till that the wearer's very means do ebb?
What woman in the city do I name

When that I say the city-woman bears

The cost of princes on unworthy shoulders?

Who can come in and say that I mean her,

When such a one as she such is herneighbour?

Or what is he of basest function

That says his bravery is not on my cost,

Thinking that I mean him, but therein suits

His folly to the mettle of my speech?

There then! how then? what then? Let me see wherein

My tongue hathwrong'd him: if it do him right,

Then he hathwrong'd himself; if he be free,

Why then my taxing like a wild-goose flies,

Unclaim'd of any man. But who comes here?

[*Enter ORLANDO with his sword drawn*]

ORLANDO:

Forbear, and eat no more.

JAQUES:

Why, I have eat none yet.

ORLANDO:

Norshalt not, till necessity be serv'd.

JAQUES:

Of what kind should this cock come of?

DUKE SENIOR:

Art thou thusbolden'd, man, by thy distress?
Or else a rude despiser of good manners,
That in civility thouseem'st so empty?

ORLANDO:

Youtouch'd my vein at first: the thorny point
Of bare distress hathta'en from me the show
Of smooth civility; yetarn I inland bred,
And know some nurture. But forbear, I say;
He dies that touches any of this fruit
Till I and my affairs are answered.

JAQUES:

An you will not beanswer'd with reason, I must die.

DUKE SENIOR:

What would you have? Your gentleness shall force
More than your force move us to gentleness.

ORLANDO:

I almost die for food, and let me have it.

DUKE SENIOR:

Sit down and feed, and welcome to our table.

ORLANDO:

Speak you so gently? Pardon me, I pray you;

I thought that all things had been savage here,
And therefore put I on the countenance
Of stern commandment. Butwhate'er you are
That in this desert inaccessible,
Under the shade of melancholy boughs,
Lose and neglect the creeping hours of time;
If ever you havelook'd on better days,
If ever been where bells haveknoll'd to church,
If ever sat at any good man's feast,
If ever from your eyelidswip'd a tear,
And know what 'tis to pity and be pitied,
Let gentleness my strong enforcement be;
In the which hope I blush, and hide my sword.

DUKE SENIOR:

True is it that we have seen better days,
And have with holy bell beenknoll'd to church,
And sat at good men's feasts, andwip'd our eyes
Of drops that sacred pity hathengend'red;
And therefore sit you down in gentleness,
And take upon command what help we have
That to your wanting may beminist'red.

ORLANDO:

Then but forbear your food a little while,

Whiles, like a doe, I go to find my fawn,

And give it food. There is an old poor man

Who after me hath many a weary step

Limp'd in pure love; till he be first suffic'd,

Oppress'd with two weak evils, age and hunger,

I will not touch a bit.

DUKE SENIOR:

Go find him out.

And we will nothing waste till you return.

ORLANDO:

I thank ye; and beblest for your good comfort!

[*Exit*]

DUKE SENIOR:

Thouseest we are not all alone unhappy:

This wide and universal theatre

Presents more woeful pageants than the scene

Wherein we play in.

JAQUES:

All the world's a stage,

And all the men and women merely players;

They have their exits and their entrances;

And one man in his time plays many parts,
His acts being seven ages. At first the infant,
Mewling and puking in the nurse's arms;
Then the whining school-boy, with his satchel
And shining morning face, creeping like snail
Unwillingly to school. And then the lover,
Sighing like furnace, with a woeful ballad
Made to his mistress' eyebrow. Then a soldier,
Full of strange oaths, and bearded like thepard,
Jealous inhonour, sudden and quick in quarrel,
Seeking the bubble reputation
Even in the cannon's mouth. And then the justice,
In fair round belly with good caponlin'd,
With eyes severe and beard of formal cut,
Full of wise saws and modern instances;
And so he plays his part. The sixth age shifts
Into the lean andslipper'd pantaloon,
With spectacles on nose and pouch on side,
His youthful hose, wellsav'd, a world too wide
For his shrunk shank; and his big manly voice,
Turning again toward childish treble, pipes
And whistles in his sound. Last scene of all,
That ends this strange eventful history,

Is second childishness and mere oblivion;

Sans teeth, sans eyes, sans taste, sansevery thing.

[*Re-enter ORLANDO with ADAM*]

DUKE SENIOR:

Welcome. Set down your venerable burden.

And let him feed.

ORLANDO:

I thank you most for him.

ADAM:

So had you need;

I scarce can speak to thank you for myself.

DUKE SENIOR:

Welcome; fall to. I will not trouble you

As yet to question you about your fortunes.

Give us some music; and, good cousin, sing.

[*SONG*]

Blow, blow, thou winter wind,

Thou art not so unkind

As man's ingratitude;

Thy tooth is not so keen,

Because thou art not seen,

Although thy breath be rude.

Heigh-ho! sing heigh-ho! unto the green holly.

Most friendship is feigning, most loving mere folly.

Then, heigh-ho, the holly!

This life is most jolly.

Freeze, freeze, thou bitter sky,

That dost not bite so nigh

As benefits forgot;

Though thou the waters warp,

Thy sting is not so sharp

As friendrememb'red not.

Heigh-ho! sing, &c.

DUKE SENIOR:

If that you were the good Sir Rowland's son,

As you havewhisper'd faithfully you were,

And as mine eye doth his effigies witness

Most trulylimn'd and living in your face,

Be truly welcome hither. I am the Duke

Thatlov'd your father. The residue of your fortune,

Go to my cave and tell me. Good old man,

Thou art right welcome as thy master is.

Support him by the arm. Give me your hand,
And let me all your fortunes understand.

[*Exeunt*]

ACT 3.

SCENE I.
The palace

[*Enter DUKE FREDERICK, OLIVER, and LORDS*]

FREDERICK:
Not see him since! Sir, sir, that cannot be.
But were I not the better part made mercy,
I should not seek an absent argument
Of my revenge, thou present. But look to it:
Find out thy brotherwheresoe'er he is;
Seek him with candle; bring him dead or living
Within this twelvemonth, or turn thou no more
To seek a living in our territory.

Thy lands and all things that thou dost callthine
Worth seizure do we seize into our hands,
Till thou canst quit thee by thy brother's mouth
Of what we think against thee.

OLIVER:

O that your Highness knew my heart in this!
I neverlov'd my brother in my life.

FREDERICK:

More villain thou. Well, push him out of doors;
And let my officers of such a nature
Make an extent upon his house and lands.
Do this expediently, and turn him going.

[*Exeunt*]

SCENE II.
The forest

[*Enter ORLANDO, with a paper*]

ORLANDO:

Hang there, my verse, in witness of my love;
And thou, thrice-crowned Queen of Night, survey
With thy chaste eye, from thy pale sphere above,
Thy huntress' name that my full life doth sway.
O Rosalind! these trees shall be my books,
And in their barks my thoughts I'll character,
That every eye which in this forest looks
Shall see thy virtuewitness'd every where.
Run, run, Orlando; carve on every tree,
The fair, the chaste, and unexpressive she.

[*Exit*]

[*Enter CORIN and TOUCHSTONE*]

CORIN:
And how like you this shepherd's life, Master Touchstone?
TOUCHSTONE:
Truly, shepherd, in respect of itself, it is a good life; but in respect that it is a shepherd's life, it isnought. In respect that it is solitary, I like it very well; but in respect that it is private, it is a very vile life. Now in respect it is in the fields, itpleaseth me well; but in respect it is not in the court, it is

tedious. As it is a spare life, look you, it fits myhumour well; but as there is no more plenty in it, it goes much against my stomach. Hast any philosophy in thee, shepherd?

CORIN:

No more but that I know the more one sickens the worse at ease he is; and that he that wants money, means, and content, is without three good friends; that the property of rain is to wet, and fire to burn; that good pasture makes fat sheep; and that a great cause of the night is lack of the sun; that he that hath learned no wit by nature nor art may complain of good breeding, or comes of a very dull kindred.

TOUCHSTONE:

Such a one is a natural philosopher. Wast ever in court, shepherd?

CORIN:

No, truly.

TOUCHSTONE:

Then thou artdamn'd.

CORIN:

Nay, I hope.

TOUCHSTONE:

Truly, thou artdamn'd, like an ill-roasted egg, all on one side.

CORIN:

For not being at court? Your reason.

TOUCHSTONE:

Why, if thou neverwast at court thou never saw'st good manners; if thou neversaw'st good manners, then thy manners must be wicked; and wickedness is sin, and sin is damnation. Thou art in a parlous state, shepherd.

CORIN:

Not a whit, Touchstone. Those that are good manners at the court are as ridiculous in the country as thebehaviour of the country is mostmockable at the court. You told me you salute not at the court, but you kiss your hands; that courtesy would be uncleanly if courtiers were shepherds.

TOUCHSTONE:

Instance, briefly; come, instance.

CORIN:

Why, we are still handling our ewes; and their fells, you know, are greasy.

TOUCHSTONE:

Why, do not your courtier's hands sweat? And is not the grease of a mutton as wholesome as the sweat of a man? Shallow, shallow. A better instance, I say; come.

CORIN:

Besides, our hands are hard.

TOUCHSTONE:

Your lips will feel them the sooner. Shallow again.

A more sounder instance; come.

CORIN:

And they are oftentarr'd over with the surgery of our sheep; and would you have us kiss tar? The courtier's hands are perfum'd with civet.

TOUCHSTONE:

Most shallow man! thou worm's meat in respect of a good piece of flesh indeed! Learn of the wise, andperpend: civet is of a baser birth than tar- the very uncleanly flux of a cat. Mend the instance, shepherd.

CORIN:

You have too courtly a wit for me; I'll rest.

TOUCHSTONE:

Wilt thou restdamn'd? God help thee, shallow man!
God make incision in thee! thou art raw.

CORIN:

Sir, I am a truelabourer: I earn that I eat, get that I
wear; owe no man hate, envy no man's happiness; glad of other

men's good, content with my harm; and the greatest of my

pride is

to see my ewes graze and my lambs suck.

TOUCHSTONE:

That is another simple sin in you: to bring the ewes and the rams together, and to offer to get your living by the copulation of cattle; to be bawd to a bell-wether, and to betray a she-lamb of a twelvemonth to crooked-pated, old, cuckoldly ram, out of all reasonable match. If thoubeest not damn'd for this, the devil himself will have no shepherds; I cannot see else how thoushouldst scape.

CORIN:

Here comes young Master Ganymede, my new mistress's brother.

[*Enter ROSALIND, reading a paper*]

ROSALIND:

'From the east to westernInde,

No jewel is likeRosalinde.

Her worth, being mounted on the wind,

Through all the world bearsRosalinde.

All the pictures fairestlin'd

Are but black toRosalinde.

Let no face be kept in mind

But the fair ofRosalinde.'

TOUCHSTONE:

I'll rhyme you so eight years together, dinners, and suppers, and sleeping hours, excepted. It is the right butter-women's rank to market.

ROSALIND:

Out, fool!

TOUCHSTONE:

For a taste:

If a hart do lack a hind,

Let him seek outRosalinde.

If the cat will after kind,

So be sure willRosalinde.

Winter garments must belin'd,

So must slenderRosalinde.

They that reap must sheaf and bind,

Then to cart withRosalinde.

Sweetest nut hath sourest rind,

Such a nut isRosalinde.

He that sweetest rose will find

Must find love's prick andRosalinde.

This is the very false gallop of verses; why do you infect yourself with them?

ROSALIND:

Peace, you dull fool! I found them on a tree.

TOUCHSTONE:

Truly, the tree yields bad fruit.

ROSALIND:

I'llgraff it with you, and then I shall graff it with a medlar. Then it will be the earliest fruit i' th' country; for you'll be rotten ere you be half ripe, and that's the right virtue of themedlar.

TOUCHSTONE:

You have said; but whether wisely or no, let the forest judge.

[*Enter CELIA, with a writing*]

ROSALIND:

Peace!

Here comes my sister, reading; stand aside.

CELIA:

'Why should this a desert be?

For it isunpeopled? No;

Tongues I'll hang on every tree

That shall civil sayings show.

Some, how brief the life of man
Runs his erring pilgrimage,
That thestreching of a span
Buckles in his sum of age;
Some, of violated vows
'Twixt the souls of friend and friend;
But upon the fairest boughs,
Or at every sentence end,
Will I Rosalinda write,
Teaching all that read to know
The quintessence of every sprite
Heaven would in little show.
Therefore heaven Naturecharg'd
That one body should befill'd
With all graces wide-enlarg'd.
Nature presentlydistill'd
Helen's cheek, but not her heart,
Cleopatra's majesty,
Atalanta's better part,
SadLucretia's modesty.
ThusRosalinde of many parts
By heavenly synod wasdevis'd,
Of many faces, eyes, and hearts,

To have the touches dearestpriz'd.

Heaven would that she these gifts should have,

And I to live and die her slave.'

ROSALIND:

O most gentlepulpiter! What tedious homily of love have you wearied your parishioners withal, and never cried 'Have patience, good people.'

CELIA:

How now! Back, friends; shepherd, go off a little; go with him, sirrah.

TOUCHSTONE:

Come, shepherd, let us make anhonourable retreat; though not with bag and baggage, yet with scrip andscrippage.

[*Exeunt CORIN and TOUCHSTONE*]

CELIA:

Didst thou hear these verses?

ROSALIND:

O, yes, I heard them all, and more too; for some of them had in them more feet than the verses would bear.

CELIA:

That's no matter; the feet might bear the verses.

ROSALIND:

Ay, but the feet were lame, and could not bear themselves without the verse, and therefore stood lamely in the verse.

CELIA:

But didst thou hear without wondering how thy name should be hang'd and carved upon these trees?

ROSALIND:

I was seven of the nine days out of the wonder before you came; for look here what I found on a palm-tree. I was never so berhym'd since Pythagoras' time that I was an Irish rat, which I can hardly remember.

CELIA:

Trow you who hath done this?

ROSALIND:

Is it a man?

CELIA:

And a chain, that you once wore, about his neck.
Change youcolour?

ROSALIND:

Iprithee, who?

CELIA:

O Lord, Lord! it is a hard matter for friends to meet; but mountains may beremov'd with earthquakes, and so encounter.

ROSALIND:

Nay, but who is it?

CELIA:

Is it possible?

ROSALIND:

Nay, Iprithee now, with most petitionary vehemence, tell me who it is.

CELIA:

O wonderful, wonderful, most wonderfulwonderful, and yet again wonderful, and after that, out of all whooping!

ROSALIND:

Good my complexion! dost thou think, though I am caparison'd like a man, I have a doublet and hose in my disposition? One inch of delay more is a South Sea of discovery.

Iprithee tell me who is it quickly, and speak apace. I would thoucould'st stammer, that thou mightst pour this conceal'd man out of thy mouth, as wine comes out of narrow-mouth'd bottle- either too much at once or none at all. Iprithee take the cork out of thy mouth that I may drink thy tidings.

CELIA:

So you may put a man in your belly.

ROSALIND:

Is he of God's making? What manner of man?
Is his head worth a hat or his chin worth a beard?

CELIA:

Nay, he hath but a little beard.

ROSALIND:

Why, God will send more if the man will be thankful.
Let me stay the growth of his beard, if thou delay me not the knowledge of his chin.

CELIA:

It is young Orlando, thattripp'd up the wrestler's heels and your heart both in an instant.

ROSALIND:

Nay, but the devil take mocking! Speak sad brow and true maid.

CELIA:

I' faith, coz, 'tis he.

ROSALIND:

Orlando?

CELIA:

Orlando.

ROSALIND:

Alas the day! what shall I do with my doublet and hose?

What did he when thousaw'st him? What said he? How look'd he?

Wherein went he? What makes he here? Did he ask for me? Where remains he? How parted he with thee? And whenshalt thou see him again? Answer me in one word.

CELIA:

You must borrow meGargantua's mouth first; 'tis a word too great for any mouth of this age's size. To say ay and no to these particulars is more than to answer in a catechism.

ROSALIND:

But doth he know that I am in this forest, and in man's apparel? Looks he as freshly as he did the day he wrestled?

CELIA:

It is as easy to count atomies as to resolve the propositions of a lover; but take a taste of my finding him, and relish it with good observance. I found him under a tree, like a dropp'd acorn.

ROSALIND:

It may well becall'd Jove's tree, when it drops forth such fruit.

CELIA:

Give me audience, good madam.

ROSALIND:

Proceed.

CELIA:

There lay he, stretch'd along like a wounded knight.

ROSALIND:

Though it be pity to see such a sight, it well becomes the ground.

CELIA:

Cry 'Holla' to thy tongue, I prithee; it curvets unseasonably. He wasfurnish'd like a hunter.

ROSALIND:

O, ominous! he comes to kill my heart.

CELIA:

I would sing my song without a burden; thoubring'st me out of tune.

ROSALIND:

Do you not know I am a woman? When I think, I must speak.

Sweet, say on.

CELIA:

You bring me out. Soft! comes he not here?

[*Enter ORLANDO and JAQUES*]

ROSALIND:

'Tis he; slink by, and note him.

JAQUES:

I thank you for your company; but, good faith, I had as lief have been myself alone.

ORLANDO:

And so had I; but yet, for fashion sake, I thank you too for your society.

JAQUES:

God buy you; let's meet as little as we can.

ORLANDO:

I do desire we may be better strangers.

JAQUES:

I pray you mar no more trees with writing love songs in their barks.

ORLANDO:

I pray you mar no more of my verses with reading them ill-favouredly.

JAQUES:

Rosalind is your love's name?

ORLANDO:

Yes, just.

JAQUES:

I do not like her name.

ORLANDO:

There was no thought of pleasing you when she was christen'd.

JAQUES:

What stature is she of?

ORLANDO:

Just as high as my heart.

JAQUES:

You are full of pretty answers. Have you not been acquainted with goldsmiths' wives, andconn'd them out of rings?

ORLANDO:

Not so; but I answer you right painted cloth, from whence you have studied your questions.

JAQUES:

You have a nimble wit; I think 'twas made ofAtalanta's heels. Will you sit down with me? and we two will rail against our mistress the world, and all our misery.

ORLANDO:

I will chide no breather in the world but myself, against whom I know most faults.

JAQUES:

The worst fault you have is to be in love.

ORLANDO:

'Tis a fault I will not change for your best virtue. I am weary of you.

JAQUES:

By my troth, I was seeking for a fool when I found you.

ORLANDO:

He isdrown'd in the brook; look but in, and you shall see him.

JAQUES:

There I shall see mine own figure.

ORLANDO:

Which I take to be either a fool or a cipher.

JAQUES:

I'll tarry no longer with you; farewell, goodSignior Love.

ORLANDO:

I am glad of your departure; adieu, good Monsieur Melancholy.

[*Exit JAQUES*]

ROSALIND:

[*Aside to CELIA*] I will speak to him like a saucy lackey, and under that habit play the knave with him. - Do you hear, forester?

ORLANDO:

Very well; what would you?

ROSALIND:

I pray you, whatis't o'clock?

ORLANDO:

You should ask me what time o' day; there's no clock in the forest.

ROSALIND:

Then there is no true lover in the forest, else sighing every minute and groaning every hour would detect the lazy foot of Time as well as a clock.

ORLANDO:

And why not the swift foot of Time? Had not that been as proper?

ROSALIND:

By no means, sir. Time travels in divers paces with divers persons. I'll tell you who Time ambles withal, who Time trots withal, who Time gallops withal, and who he stands still withal.

ORLANDO:

Iprithee, who doth he trot withal?

ROSALIND:

Marry, he trots hard with a young maid between the contract of her marriage and the day it issolemniz'd; if the interim be but ase'nnight, Time's pace is so hard that it seems the length of seven year.

ORLANDO:

Who ambles Time withal?

ROSALIND:

With a priest that lacks Latin and a rich man that hath not the gout; for the one sleeps easily because he cannot study, and the other lives merrily because he feels no pain; the one lacking the burden of lean and wasteful learning, the other knowing no burden of heavy tedious penury. These Time ambles withal.

ORLANDO:

Who doth he gallop withal?

ROSALIND:

With a thief to the gallows; for though he go as softly as foot can fall, he thinks himself too soon there.

ORLANDO:

Who stays it still withal?

ROSALIND:

With lawyers in the vacation; for they sleep between term and term, and then they perceive not how Time moves.

ORLANDO:

Where dwell you, pretty youth?

ROSALIND:

With this shepherdess, my sister; here in the skirts of the forest, like fringe upon a petticoat.

ORLANDO:

Are you native of this place?

ROSALIND:

As theconey that you see dwell where she is kindled.

ORLANDO:

Your accent is something finer than you could purchase in so removed a dwelling.

ROSALIND:

I have been told so of many; but indeed an old religious uncle of mine taught me to speak, who was in his youth an inland man; one that knew courtship too well, for there he fell in love.

I have heard him read many lectures against it; and I thank God I am not a woman, to betouch'd with so many giddy offences as he hath generallytax'd their whole sex withal.

ORLANDO:

Can you remember any of the principal evils that he laid to the charge of women?

ROSALIND:

There were none principal; they were all like one another as halfpence are; every one fault seeming monstrous till his fellow-fault came to match it.

ORLANDO:

Iprithee recount some of them.

ROSALIND:

No; I will not cast away my physic but on those that are sick. There is a man haunts the forest that abuses our young plants with carving 'Rosalind' on their barks; hangs odes upon hawthorns and elegies on brambles; all, forsooth, deifying the name of Rosalind. If I could meet that fancy-monger, I would give him some good counsel, for he seems to have the quotidian of love upon him.

ORLANDO:

I am he that is so love-shak'd; I pray you tell me your remedy.

ROSALIND:

There is none of my uncle's marks upon you; he taught me how to know a man in love; in which cage of rushes I am sure you are not prisoner.

ORLANDO:

What were his marks?

ROSALIND:

A lean cheek, which you have not; a blue eye and sunken, which you have not; an unquestionable spirit, which you have not; a beard neglected, which you have not; but I pardon you for that, for simply your having in beard is a younger brother's revenue.

Then your hose should beungarter'd, your bonnet unbanded, your sleeveunbutton'd, your shoe untied, and every thing about you demonstrating a careless desolation. But you are no such man; you are rather point-device in your accoutrements, as loving yourself than seeming the lover of any other.

ORLANDO:

Fair youth, I would I could make thee believe I love.

ROSALIND:

Me believe it! You may as soon make her that you love believe it; which, I warrant, she isapter to do than to confess she does. That is one of the points in the which women still give the lie to their consciences. But, in good sooth, are you he that hangs the verses on the trees wherein Rosalind is so admired?

ORLANDO:

I swear to thee, youth, by the white hand of Rosalind, I am that he, that unfortunate he.

ROSALIND:

But are you so much in love as your rhymes speak?

ORLANDO:

Neither rhyme nor reason can express how much.

ROSALIND:

Love is merely a madness; and, I tell you, deserves as well a dark house and a whip as madmen do; and the reason why they are not sopunish'd and cured is that the lunacy is so ordinary that thewhippers are in love too. Yet I profess curing it by counsel.

ORLANDO:

Did you ever cure any so?

ROSALIND:

Yes, one; and in this manner. He was to imagine me his love, his mistress; and I set him every day to woo me; at which time would I, being but amoonish youth, grieve, be effeminate, changeable, longing and liking, proud, fantastical, apish, shallow, inconstant, full of tears, full of smiles; for every passion something and for no passion truly anything, as boys and women are for the most part cattle of thiscolour; would now like him, now loathe him; then entertain him, then forswear him; now weep for him, then spit at him; that Idrave my suitor from his madhumour of love to a living humour of madness; which was, to forswear the full stream of the world and to live in a nook merely monastic. And thus I cur'd him; and this way will I take upon me to wash your liver as clean as a sound sheep's heart, that there shall not be one spot of love in 't.

ORLANDO:

I would not be cured, youth.

ROSALIND:

I would cure you, if you would but call me Rosalind, and come every day to mycote and woo me.

ORLANDO:

Now, by the faith of my love, I will. Tell me where it is.

ROSALIND:

Go with me to it, and I'll show it you; and, by the way, you shall tell me where in the forest you live. Will you go?

ORLANDO:

With all my heart, good youth.

ROSALIND:

Nay, you must call me Rosalind. Come, sister, will you go?

[*Exeunt*]

SCENE III.
The forest

[*Enter TOUCHSTONE and AUDREY; JAQUES behind*]

TOUCHSTONE:

Come apace, good Audrey; I will fetch up your goats, Audrey. And how, Audrey, am I the man yet? Doth my simple feature content you?

AUDREY:

Your features! Lord warrant us! What features?

TOUCHSTONE:

I am here with thee and thy goats, as the most capricious poet, honest Ovid, was among the Goths.

JAQUES:

[*Aside*] O knowledge ill-inhabited, worse than Jove in a thatch'd house!

TOUCHSTONE:

When a man's verses cannot be understood, nor a man's good wit seconded with the forward child understanding, it strikes a man more dead than a great reckoning in a little room.

Truly, I would the gods had made thee poetical.

AUDREY:

I do not know what 'poetical' is. Is it honest in deed and word? Is it a true thing?

TOUCHSTONE:

No, truly; for the truest poetry is the most feigning, and lovers are given to poetry; and what they swear in poetry may be said as lovers they do feign.

AUDREY:

Do you wish, then, that the gods had made me poetical?

TOUCHSTONE:

I do, truly, for thouswear'st to me thou art honest; now, if thou wert a poet, I might have some hope thou didst feign.

AUDREY:

Would you not have me honest?

TOUCHSTONE:

No, truly, unless thou wert hard-favour'd; for honesty coupled to beauty is to have honey a sauce to sugar.

JAQUES:

[*Aside*] A material fool!

AUDREY:

Well, I am not fair; and therefore I pray the gods make me honest.

TOUCHSTONE:

Truly, and to cast away honesty upon a foul slut were to put good meat into an unclean dish.

AUDREY:

I am not a slut, though I thank the gods I am foul.

TOUCHSTONE:

Well, praised be the gods for thy foulness; sluttishness may come hereafter. But be it as it may be, I will marry thee; and to that end I have been with Sir OliverMartext, the vicar of the next village, who hathpromis'd to meet me in this place of the forest, and to couple us.

JAQUES:

[*Aside*] I would fain see this meeting.

AUDREY:

Well, the gods give us joy!

TOUCHSTONE:

Amen. A man may, if he were of a fearful heart, stagger in this attempt; for here we have no temple but the wood, no assembly but horn-beasts. But what though? Courage! As horns are odious, they are necessary. It is said: 'Many a man knows no end of his goods.' Right! Many a man has good horns and knows no end of them. Well, that is the dowry of his wife; 'tis none of his own getting. Horns? Even so. Poor men alone? No, no; the noblest deer hath them as huge as the rascal. Is the single man therefore blessed? No; as awall'd town is more worthier than a village, so is the forehead of a married man morehonourable than the bare brow of a bachelor; and by how muchdefence is better than no skill, by so much is horn more precious than to want. Here comes Sir Oliver.

[*Enter SIR OLIVER MARTEXT*]

Sir OliverMartext, you are well met. Will you dispatch us here under this tree, or shall we go with you to your chapel?
MARTEXT:
Is there none here to give the woman?
TOUCHSTONE:
I will not take her on gift of any man.
MARTEXT:
Truly, she must be given, or the marriage is not lawful.
JAQUES:
[*Discovering himself*] Proceed, proceed; I'll give her.
TOUCHSTONE:
Good even, good Master What-ye-call't; how do you, sir? You are very well met. Goddild you for your last company. I

am very glad to see you. Even a toy in hand here, sir. Nay; pray be cover'd.

JAQUES:

Will you be married, motley?

TOUCHSTONE:

As the ox hath his bow, sir, the horse his curb, and the falcon her bells, so man hath his desires; and as pigeons bill, so wedlock would be nibbling.

JAQUES:

And will you, being a man of your breeding, be married under a bush, like a beggar? Get you to church and have a good priest that can tell you what marriage is; this fellow will but join you together as they join wainscot; then one of you will prove a shrunk panel, and like green timber warp, warp.

TOUCHSTONE:

[*Aside*] I am not in the mind but I were better to be married of him than of another; for he is not like to marry me well; and not being well married, it will be a good excuse for me hereafter to leave my wife.

JAQUES:

Gothou with me, and let me counsel thee.

TOUCHSTONE:

Come, sweet Audrey;

We must be married or we must live in bawdry.

Farewell, good Master Oliver. Not-

O sweet Oliver,

O brave Oliver,

Leave me not behind thee.

But-

Wind away,

Begone, I say,

I will not to wedding with thee.

[*Exeunt JAQUES, TOUCHSTONE, and AUDREY*]

MARTEXT:

'Tis no matter; ne'er a fantastical knave of them all shall flout me out of my calling.

[*Exit*]

SCENE IV.
The forest

[*Enter ROSALIND and CELIA*]

ROSALIND:

Never talk to me; I will weep.

CELIA:

Do, Iprithee; but yet have the grace to consider that tears do not become a man.

ROSALIND:

But have I not cause to weep?

CELIA:

As good cause as one would desire; therefore weep.

ROSALIND:

His very hair is of the dissemblingcolour.

CELIA:

Something browner than Judas's.

Marry, his kisses are Judas's own children.

ROSALIND:

I' faith, his hair is of a goodcolour.

CELIA:

An excellentcolour; your chestnut was ever the only colour.

ROSALIND:

And his kissing is as full of sanctity as the touch of holy bread.

CELIA:

He hath bought a pair of cast lips of Diana. A nun of winter's sisterhood kisses not more religiously; the very ice of chastity is in them.

ROSALIND:

But why did he swear he would come this morning, and comes not?

CELIA:

Nay, certainly, there is no truth in him.

ROSALIND:

Do you think so?

CELIA:

Yes; I think he is not a pick-purse nor a horse-stealer; but for his verity in love, I do think him as concave as covered goblet or a worm-eaten nut.

ROSALIND:

Not true in love?

CELIA:

Yes, when he is in; but I think he is not in.

ROSALIND:

You have heard him swear downright he was.

CELIA:

'Was' is not 'is'; besides, the oath of a lover is no stronger than the word of a tapster; they are both the confirmer of false reckonings. He attends here in the forest on the Duke, your father.

ROSALIND:

I met the Duke yesterday, and had much question with him. He asked me of what parentage I was; I told him, of as good as he; so helaugh'd and let me go. But what talk we of fathers when there is such a man as Orlando?

CELIA:

O, that's a brave man! He writes brave verses, speaks brave words, swears brave oaths, and breaks them bravely, quite traverse, athwart the heart of his lover; as a puny tilter, that spurs his horse but on one side, breaks his staff like a noble goose. But all's brave that youth mounts and folly guides. Who comes here?

[*Enter CORIN*]

CORIN:

Mistress and master, you have oft enquired
After the shepherd thatcomplain'd of love,
Who you saw sitting by me on the turf,
Praising the proud disdainful shepherdess
That was his mistress.

CELIA:

Well, and what of him?

CORIN:

If you will see a pageant trulyplay'd
Between the pale complexion of true love
And the red glow of scorn and proud disdain,
Go hence a little, and I shall conduct you,
If you will mark it.

ROSALIND:

O, come, let us remove!
The sight of loversfeedeth those in love.
Bring us to this sight, and you shall say
I'll prove a busy actor in their play.

[*Exeunt*]

SCENE V.
Another part of the forest

[*Enter SILVIUS and PHEBE*]

SILVIUS:

    SweetPhebe, do not scorn me; do not, Phebe.
    Say that you love me not; but say not so
    In bitterness. The common executioner,
    Whose heartth' accustom'd sight of death makes hard,
    Falls not the axe upon the humbled neck
    But first begs pardon. Will you sterner be
    Than he that dies and lives by bloody drops?

[*Enter ROSALIND, CELIA, and CORIN, at a distance*]

PHEBE:

    I would not be thy executioner;
    I fly thee, for I would not injure thee.
    Thoutell'st me there is murder in mine eye.
    'Tis pretty, sure, and very probable,

That eyes, that are thefrail'st and softest things,
Who shut their coward gates on atomies,
Should becall'd tyrants, butchers, murderers!
Now I do frown on thee with all my heart;
And if mine eyes can wound, now let them kill thee.
Now counterfeit to swoon; why, now fall down;
Or, if thou canst not, O, for shame, for shame,
Lie not, to say mine eyes are murderers.
Now show the wound mine eye hath made in thee.
Scratch thee but with a pin, and there remains
Some scar of it; lean upon a rush,
Thecicatrice and capable impressure
Thy palm some moment keeps; but now mine eyes,
Which I have darted at thee, hurt thee not;
Nor, I am sure, there is not force in eyes
That can do hurt.

SILVIUS:

O dearPhebe,
If ever- as that ever may be near-
You meet in some fresh cheek the power of fancy,
Then shall you know the wounds invisible
That love's keen arrows make.

PHEBE:

But till that time

Come not thou near me; and when that time comes,

Afflict me with thy mocks, pity me not;

As till that time I shall not pity thee.

ROSALIND:

[*Advancing*] And why, I pray you? Who might be your mother,

That you insult, exult, and all at once,

Over the wretched? What though you have no beauty-

As, by my faith, I see no more in you

Than without candle may go dark to bed-

Must you be therefore proud and pitiless?

Why, what means this? Why do you look on me?

I see no more in you than in the ordinary

Of nature's sale-work. 'Od's my little life,

I think she means to tangle my eyes too!

No faith, proud mistress, hope not after it;

'Tis not your inky brows, your black silk hair,

Your bugle eyeballs, nor your cheek of cream,

That canentame my spirits to your worship.

You foolish shepherd, wherefore do you follow her,

Like foggy south, puffing with wind and rain?

You are a thousand times aproperer man

Than she a woman. 'Tis such fools as you
That makes the world full of ill-favour'd children.
'Tis not her glass, but you, that flatters her;
And out of you she sees herself more proper
Than any of her lineaments can show her.
But, mistress, know yourself. Down on your knees,
And thank heaven, fasting, for a good man's love;
For I must tell you friendly in your ear:
Sell when you can; you are not for all markets.
Cry the man mercy, love him, take his offer;
Foul is most foul, being foul to be a scoffer.
So take her to thee, shepherd. Fare you well.

PHEBE:

Sweet youth, I pray you chide a year together;
I had rather hear you chide than this man woo.

ROSALIND:

He's fall'n in love with your foulness, and she'll fall in love with my anger. If it be so, as fast as she answers thee with frowning looks, I'll sauce her with bitter words. Why look you so upon me?

PHEBE:

For no ill will I bear you.

ROSALIND:

I pray you do not fall in love with me,
For I am falser than vows made in wine;
Besides, I like you not. If you will know my house,
'Tis at the tuft of olives here hard by.
Will you go, sister? Shepherd, ply her hard.
Come, sister. Shepherdess, look on him better,
And be not proud; though all the world could see,
None could be soabus'd in sight as he.
Come, to our flock.

[*Exeunt ROSALIND, CELIA, and CORIN*]

PHEBE:

Dead shepherd, now I findthy saw of might:
'Who everlov'd that lov'd not at first sight?'

SILVIUS:

SweetPhebe.

PHEBE:

Ha! whatsay'st thou, Silvius?

SILVIUS:

SweetPhebe, pity me.

PHEBE:

Why, Iarn sorry for thee, gentle Silvius.

SILVIUS:

Wherever sorrow is, relief would be.
If you do sorrow at my grief in love,
By giving love, your sorrow and my grief
Were bothextermin'd.

PHEBE:

Thou hast my love; is not thatneighbourly?

SILVIUS:

I would have you.

PHEBE:

Why, that were covetousness.
Silvius, the time was that I hated thee;
And yet it is not that I bear thee love;
But since that thou canst talk of love so well,
Thy company, whicherst was irksome to me,
I will endure; and I'll employ thee too.
But do not look for further recompense
Thanthine own gladness that thou art employ'd.

SILVIUS:

So holy and so perfect is my love,
And I in such a poverty of grace,
That I shall think it a most plenteous crop
To glean the broken ears after the man

That the main harvest reaps; loose now and then
A scatt'red smile, and that I'll live upon.
PHEBE:
Know'st thou the youth that spoke to me erewhile?
SILVIUS:
Not very well; but I have met him oft;
And he hath bought the cottage and the bounds
That the old carlot once was master of.
PHEBE:
Think not I love him, though I ask for him;
'Tis but a peevish boy; yet he talks well.
But what care I for words? Yet words do well
When he that speaks them pleases those that hear.
It is a pretty youth- not very pretty;
But, sure, he's proud; and yet his pride becomes him.
He'll make a proper man. The best thing in him
Is his complexion; and faster than his tongue
Did make offence, his eye did heal it up.
He is not very tall; yet for his years he's tall;
His leg is but so-so; and yet 'tis well.
There was a pretty redness in his lip,
A little riper and more lusty red
Than that mix'd in his cheek; 'twas just the difference

Betwixt the constant red and mingled damask.
There be some women, Silvius, had they mark'd him
In parcels as I did, would have gone near
To fall in love with him; but, for my part,
I love him not, nor hate him not; and yet
I have more cause to hate him than to love him;
For what had he to do to chide at me?
He said mine eyes were black, and my hair black,
And, now I amrememb'red, scorn'd at me.
I marvel why Ianswer'd not again;
But that's all one: omittance is no quittance.
I'll write to him a very taunting letter,
And thoushalt bear it; wilt thou, Silvius?

SILVIUS:

Phebe, with all my heart.

PHEBE:

I'll write it straight;
The matter's in my head and in my heart;
I will be bitter with him and passing short.
Go with me, Silvius.

[*Exeunt*]

ACT 4.

SCENE I.
The forest

[*Enter ROSALIND, CELIA, and JAQUES*]

JAQUES:

Iprithee, pretty youth, let me be better acquainted with thee.

ROSALIND:

They say you are a melancholy fellow.

JAQUES:

I am so; I do love it better than laughing.

ROSALIND:

Those that are in extremity of either are abominable fellows, and betray themselves to every modern censure worse than drunkards.

JAQUES:

Why, 'tis good to be sad and say nothing.

ROSALIND:

Why then, 'tis good to be a post.

JAQUES:

I have neither the scholar's melancholy, which is emulation; nor the musician's, which is fantastical; nor the courtier's, which is proud; nor the soldier's, which is ambitious; nor the lawyer's, which is politic; nor the lady's, which is nice; nor the lover's, which is all these; but it is a melancholy of mine own, compounded of many simples, extracted from many objects, and, indeed, the sundry contemplation of my travels; in which my often rumination wraps me in a most humorous sadness.

ROSALIND:

Atraveller! By my faith, you have great reason to be sad. I fear you have sold your own lands to see other men's; then to have seen much and to have nothing is to have rich eyes and poor hands.

JAQUES:

Yes, I havegain'd my experience.

[*Enter ORLANDO*]

ROSALIND:

And your experience makes you sad. I had rather have a fool to make me merry than experience to make me sad- and to travel for it too.

ORLANDO:

Good day, and happiness, dear Rosalind!

JAQUES:

Nay, then, God buy you, an you talk in blank verse.

ROSALIND:

Farewell, MonsieurTraveller; look you lisp and wear strange suits, disable all the benefits of your own country, be out of love with your nativity, and almost chide God for making you that countenance you are; or I will scarce think you have swam in a gondola. [Exit JAQUES] Why, how now, Orlando! where have you been all this while? You a lover! An you serve me such another trick, never come in my sight more.

ORLANDO:

My fair Rosalind, I come within an hour of my promise.

ROSALIND:

Break an hour's promise in love! He that will divide a minute into a thousand parts, and break but a part of the thousand part of a minute in the affairs of love, it may be said of him that Cupid hathclapp'd him o' th' shoulder, but I'll warrant him heart-whole.

ORLANDO:

Pardon me, dear Rosalind.

ROSALIND:

Nay, an you be so tardy, come no more in my sight. I had aslief be woo'd of a snail.

ORLANDO:

Of a snail!

ROSALIND:

Ay, of a snail; for though he comes slowly, he carries his house on his head- a better jointure, I think, than you make a woman; besides, he brings his destiny with him.

ORLANDO:

What's that?

ROSALIND:

Why, horns; which such as you are fain to be beholding to your wives for; but he comes armed in his fortune, and prevents the slander of his wife.

ORLANDO:

Virtue is no horn-maker; and my Rosalind is virtuous.

ROSALIND:

And I am your Rosalind.
CELIA:
It pleases him to call you so; but he hath a Rosalind of a better leer than you.
ROSALIND:
Come, woo me, woo me; for now I am in a holidayhumour, and like enough to consent. What would you say to me now, an I were your veryvery Rosalind?
ORLANDO:
I would kiss before I spoke.
ROSALIND:
Nay, you were better speak first; and when you were gravell'd for lack of matter, you might take occasion to kiss. Very good orators, when they are out, they will spit; and for lovers lacking- God warn us! - matter, the cleanliest shift is to kiss.
ORLANDO:
How if the kiss be denied?
ROSALIND:
Then she puts you to entreaty, and there begins new matter.
ORLANDO:
Who could be out, being before his beloved mistress?
ROSALIND:
Marry, that should you, if I were your mistress; or I should

think my honesty ranker than my wit.

ORLANDO:

What, of my suit?

ROSALIND:

Not out of your apparel, and yet out of your suit. Am not I your Rosalind?

ORLANDO:

I take some joy to say you are, because I would be talking of her.

ROSALIND:

Well, in her person, I say I will not have you.

ORLANDO:

Then, in mine own person, I die.

ROSALIND:

No, faith, die by attorney. The poor world is almost six thousand years old, and in all this time there was not any man died in his own person, videlicet, in a love-cause. Troilus had his brainsdash'd out with a Grecian club; yet he did what he could to die before, and he is one of the patterns of love. Leander, he would haveliv'd many a fair year, though Hero had turn'd nun, if it had not been for a hot midsummer night; for, good youth, he went but forth to wash him in the Hellespont, and, being taken with the cramp, wasdrown'd; and the foolish chroniclers of that age found it was- Hero of Sestos. But these are all lies: men have died from time to time, and worms have eaten them, but not for love.

ORLANDO:

I would not have my right Rosalind of this mind; for, I protest, her frown might kill me.

ROSALIND:

By this hand, it will not kill a fly. But come, now I will be your Rosalind in a more coming-on disposition; and ask me what you will, I will grant it.

ORLANDO:

Then love me, Rosalind.

ROSALIND:

Yes, faith, will I, Fridays and Saturdays, and all.

ORLANDO:

And wilt thou have me?

ROSALIND:

Ay, and twenty such.

ORLANDO:

Whatsayest thou?

ROSALIND:

Are you not good?

ORLANDO:

I hope so.

ROSALIND:

Why then, can one desire too much of a good thing?

Come, sister, you shall be the priest, and marry us. Give me your hand,

Orlando. What do you say, sister?

ORLANDO:

Pray thee, marry us.

CELIA:

I cannot say the words.

ROSALIND:

You must begin 'Will you, Orlando'-

CELIA:

Go to. Will you, Orlando, have to wife this Rosalind?

ORLANDO:

I will.

ROSALIND:

Ay, but when?

ORLANDO:

Why, now; as fast as she can marry us.

ROSALIND:

Then you must say 'I take thee, Rosalind, for wife.'

ORLANDO:

I take thee, Rosalind, for wife.

ROSALIND:

I might ask you for your commission; but- I do take thee, Orlando, for my husband. There's a girl goes before the priest; and, certainly, a woman's thought runs before her actions.

ORLANDO:

So do all thoughts; they arewing'd.

ROSALIND:

Now tell me how long you would have her, after you have possess'd her.

ORLANDO:

For ever and a day.

ROSALIND:

Say 'a day' without the 'ever.' No, no, Orlando; men are April when they woo, December when they wed: maids are May when they are maids, but the sky changes when they are wives. I will be more jealous of thee than a Barbary cock-pigeon over his hen, more clamorous than a parrot against rain, more new-fangled than an ape, more giddy in my desires than a monkey. I will weep for nothing, like Diana in the fountain, and I will do that when you aredispos'd to be merry; I will laugh like a hyen, and that when thou areinclin'd to sleep.

ORLANDO:

But will my Rosalind do so?

ROSALIND:

By my life, she will do as I do.

ORLANDO:

O, but she is wise.

ROSALIND:

Or else she could not have the wit to do this. The wiser, the-waywarder. Make the doors upon a woman's wit, and it will out at the casement; shut that, and 'twill out at the key-hole; stop that, 'twill fly with the smoke out at the chimney.

ORLANDO:

A man that had a wife with such a wit, he might say 'Wit, whither wilt? ' ROSALIND. Nay, you might keep that check for it, till you met your wife's wit going to yourneighbour's bed.

ORLANDO:

And what wit could wit have to excuse that?

ROSALIND:

Marry, to say she came to seek you there. You shall never take her without her answer, unless you take her without her tongue. O, that woman that cannot make her fault her husband's occasion, let her never nurse her child herself, for

251

she will breed it like a fool!

ORLANDO:

For these two hours, Rosalind, I will leave thee.

ROSALIND:

Alas, dear love, I cannot lack thee two hours!

ORLANDO:

I must attend the Duke at dinner; by two o'clock I will be with thee again.

ROSALIND:

Ay, go your ways, go your ways. I knew what you would prove; my friends told me as much, and I thought no less. That flattering tongue of yours won me. 'Tis but one cast away, and so, come death! Two o'clock is your hour?

ORLANDO:

Ay, sweet Rosalind.

ROSALIND:

By my troth, and in good earnest, and so God mend me, and by all pretty oaths that are not dangerous, if you break one jot of your promise, or come one minute behind your hour, I will think you the most pathetical break-promise, and the most hollow lover, and the most unworthy of her you call Rosalind, that may be chosen out of the gross band of the unfaithful. Therefore beware my censure, and keep your promise.

ORLANDO:

With no less religion than if thou wert indeed my Rosalind; so, adieu.

ROSALIND:

Well, Time is the old justice that examines all such offenders, and let Time try. Adieu.

[*Exit ORLANDO*]

CELIA:

You have simplymisus'd our sex in your love-prate. We must have your doublet and hosepluck'd over your head, and show the world what the bird hath done to her own nest.

ROSALIND:

O coz, coz, coz, my pretty little coz, that thou didst know how many fathom deep I am in love! But it cannot be sounded; my affection hath an unknown bottom, like the Bay of Portugal.

CELIA:

Or rather, bottomless; that as fast as you pour affection in, it runs out.

ROSALIND:

No; that same wicked bastard of Venus, that was begot of

thought, conceiv'd of spleen, and born of madness; that blind rascally boy, that abuses every one's eyes, because his own are out- let him be judge how deep I am in love. I'll tell thee, Aliena, I cannot be out of the sight of Orlando. I'll go find a shadow, and sigh till he come.

CELIA:
And I'll sleep.

[*Exeunt*]

SCENE II.
The forest

[*Enter JAQUES and LORDS, in the habit of foresters*]

JAQUES:
Which is he that killed the deer?

LORD:
Sir, it was I.

JAQUES:
Let's present him to the Duke, like a Roman conqueror; and

it would do well to set the deer's horns upon his head for a branch of victory. Have you no song, forester, for this purpose?

LORD:

Yes, sir.

JAQUES:

Sing it; 'tis no matter how it be in tune, so it make noise enough.

[SONG.]

What shall he have thatkill'd the deer?
His leather skin and horns to wear.

[*The rest shall hear this burden:*]

Then sing him home.
Take thou no scorn to wear the horn;
It was a crest ere thouwast born.
Thy father's father wore it;
And thy father bore it.
The horn, the horn, the lusty horn,
Is not a thing to laugh to scorn.

[*Exeunt*]

SCENE III.
The forest

[*Enter ROSALIND and CELIA*]

ROSALIND:

How say you now? Is it not past two o'clock?
And here much Orlando!

CELIA:

I warrant you, with pure love and troubled brain, he hath ta'en his bow and arrows, and is gone forth- to sleep. Look, who comes here.

[*Enter SILVIUS*]

SILVIUS:

My errand is to you, fair youth;
My gentlePhebe did bid me give you this.

I know not the contents; but, as I guess

By the stern brow and waspish action

Which she did use as she was writing of it,

It bears an angrytenour. Pardon me,

I am but as a guiltless messenger.

ROSALIND:

Patience herself would startle at this letter,

And play the swaggerer. Bear this, bear all.

She says I am not fair, that I lack manners;

She calls me proud, and that she could not love me,

Were man as rare as Phoenix. 'Od's my will!

Her love is not the hare that I do hunt;

Why writes she so to me? Well, shepherd, well,

This is a letter of your own device.

SILVIUS:

No, I protest, I know not the contents;

Phebe did write it.

ROSALIND:

Come, come, you are a fool,

Andturn'd into the extremity of love.

I saw her hand; she has a leathern hand,

A freestone-colour'd hand; I verily did think

That her old gloves were on, but 'twas her hands;

She has a huswife's hand- but that's no matter.

I say she never did invent this letter;

This is a man's invention, and his hand.

SILVIUS:

Sure, it is hers.

ROSALIND:

Why, 'tis a boisterous and a cruel style;

A style for challengers. Why, she defies me,

Like Turk to Christian. Women's gentle brain

Could not drop forth such giant-rude invention,

Such Ethiope words, blacker in their effect

Than in their countenance. Will you hear the letter?

SILVIUS:

So please you, for I never heard it yet;

Yet heard too much of Phebe's cruelty.

ROSALIND:

She Phebes me: mark how the tyrant writes.

[*Reads*]

'Art thou god to shepherd turn'd,

That a maiden's heart hath burn'd? '

Can a woman rail thus?

SILVIUS:

Call you this railing?

ROSALIND:

'Why, thy godhead laid apart,
Warr'st thou with a woman's heart? '
Did you ever hear such railing?
'Whiles the eye of man did woo me,
That could do no vengeance to me. '
Meaning me a beast.
'If the scorn of your brighteyne
Have power to raise such love in mine,
Alack, in me what strange effect
Would they work in mild aspect!
Whiles youchid me, I did love;
How then might your prayers move!
He that brings this love to the
Little knows this love in me;
And by him seal up thy mind,
Whether that thy youth and kind
Will the faithful offer take
Of me and all that I can make;
Or else by him my love deny,
And then I'll study how to die. '

SILVIUS:

Call you this chiding?

CELIA:

Alas, poor shepherd!

ROSALIND:

Do you pity him? No, he deserves no pity. Wilt thou love such a woman? What, to make thee an instrument, and play false strains upon thee! Not to beendur'd! Well, go your way to her, for I see love hath made thee tame snake, and say this to her- that if she love me, I charge her to love thee; if she will not, I will never have her unless thou entreat for her. If you be a true lover, hence, and not a word; for here comes more company.

[*Exit SILVIUS*]

[*Enter OLIVER*]

OLIVER:

Good morrow, fair ones; pray you, if you know,
Where in the purlieus of this forest stands
A sheep-cotefenc'd about with olive trees?

CELIA:

West of this place, down in theneighbour bottom.
The rank of osiers by the murmuring stream
Left on your right hand brings you to the place.
But at this hour the house doth keep itself;
There's none within.

OLIVER:

If that an eye may profit by a tongue,
Then should I know you by description-
Such garments, and such years: 'The boy is fair,
Of femalefavour, and bestows himself
Like a ripe sister; the woman low,
And browner than her brother.' Are not you
The owner of the house I did inquire for?

CELIA:

It is no boast, beingask'd, to say we are.

OLIVER:

Orlando doth commend him to you both;
And to that youth he calls his Rosalind
He sends this bloody napkin. Are you he?

ROSALIND:

I am. What must we understand by this?

OLIVER:

Some of my shame; if you will know of me

What man I am, and how, and why, and where,
This handkercher was stain'd.

CELIA:

I pray you, tell it.

OLIVER:

When last the young Orlando parted from you,
He left a promise to return again
Within an hour; and, pacing through the forest,
Chewing the food of sweet and bitter fancy,
Lo, what befell! He threw his eye aside,
And mark what object did present itself.
Under an oak, whose boughs were moss'd with age,
And high top bald with dry antiquity,
A wretched ragged man, o'ergrown with hair,
Lay sleeping on his back. About his neck
A green and gilded snake had wreath'd itself,
Who with her head nimble in threats approach'd
The opening of his mouth; but suddenly,
Seeing Orlando, it unlink'd itself,
And with indented glides did slip away
Into a bush; under which bush's shade
A lioness, with udders all drawn dry,
Lay couching, head on ground, with catlike watch,

When that the sleeping man should stir; for 'tis
The royal disposition of that beast
To prey on nothing that doth seem as dead.
This seen, Orlando did approach the man,
And found it was his brother, his elder brother.

CELIA:

O, I have heard him speak of that same brother;
And he did render him the most unnatural
Thatliv'd amongst men.

OLIVER:

And well he might so do,
For well I know he was unnatural.

ROSALIND:

But, to Orlando: did he leave him there,
Food to thesuck'd and hungry lioness?

OLIVER:

Twice did he turn his back, andpurpos'd so;
But kindness, nobler ever than revenge,
And nature, stronger than his just occasion,
Made him give battle to the lioness,
Who quickly fell before him; in which hurtling
From miserable slumber Iawak'd.

CELIA:

Are you his brother?

ROSALIND:

Was't you he rescu'd?

CELIA:

Was't you that did so oft contrive to kill him?

OLIVER:

'Twas I; but 'tis not I. I do not shame
To tell you what I was, since my conversion
So sweetly tastes, being the thing I am.

ROSALIND:

But for the bloody napkin?

OLIVER:

By and by.
When from the first to last, betwixt us two,
Tears ourrecountments had most kindly bath'd,
As how I came into that desert place-
In brief, he led me to the gentle Duke,
Who gave me fresh array and entertainment,
Committing me unto my brother's love;
Who led me instantly unto his cave,
Therestripp'd himself, and here upon his arm
The lioness had torn some flesh away,
Which all this while had bled; and now he fainted,

And cried, in fainting, upon Rosalind.
Brief, Irecover'd him, bound up his wound,
And, after some small space, being strong at heart,
He sent me hither, stranger as I am,
To tell this story, that you might excuse
His broken promise, and to give this napkin,
Dy'd in his blood, unto the shepherd youth
That he in sport doth call his Rosalind.

[ROSALIND *swoons*]

CELIA:

Why, how now, Ganymede! sweet Ganymede!

OLIVER:

Many will swoon when they do look on blood.

CELIA:

There is more in it. Cousin Ganymede!

OLIVER:

Look, he recovers.

ROSALIND:

I would I were at home.

CELIA:

We'll lead you thither.

I pray you, will you take him by the arm?

OLIVER:

Be of good cheer, youth. You a man!

You lack a man's heart.

ROSALIND:

I do so, I confess it. Ah, sirrah, a body would think this was well counterfeited. I pray you tell your brother how well I counterfeited. Heigh-ho!

OLIVER:

This was not counterfeit; there is too great testimony in your complexion that it was a passion of earnest.

ROSALIND:

Counterfeit, I assure you.

OLIVER:

Well then, take a good heart and counterfeit to be a man.

ROSALIND:

So I do; but, i' faith, I should have been a woman by right.

CELIA:

Come, you look paler and paler; pray you draw homewards. Good sir, go with us.

OLIVER:

That will I, for I must bear answer back
How you excuse my brother, Rosalind.

ROSALIND:

I shall devise something; but, I pray you, commend my counterfeiting to him. Will you go?

[*Exeunt*]

ACT 5.

SCENE I.
The forest

[*Enter TOUCHSTONE and AUDREY*]

TOUCHSTONE:
  We shall find a time, Audrey; patience, gentle Audrey.
AUDREY:
  Faith, the priest was good enough, for all the old gentleman's saying.
TOUCHSTONE:
  A most wicked Sir Oliver, Audrey, a most vileMartext.
  But, Audrey, there is a youth here in the forest lays claim to you.

AUDREY:

Ay, I know who 'tis; he hath no interest in me in the world; here comes the man you mean.

[*Enter WILLIAM*]

TOUCHSTONE:

It is meat and drink to me to see a clown. By my troth, we that have good wits have much to answer for: we shall be flouting; we cannot hold.

WILLIAM:

Goodev'n, Audrey.

AUDREY:

God ye goodev'n, William.

WILLIAM:

And goodev'n to you, sir.

TOUCHSTONE:

Goodev'n, gentle friend. Cover thy head, cover thy head; nay, prithee be cover'd. How old are you, friend?

WILLIAM:

Five and twenty, sir.

TOUCHSTONE:

A ripe age. Is thy name William?

WILLIAM:

William, sir.

TOUCHSTONE:

A fair name. Wast born i' th' forest here?

WILLIAM:

Ay, sir, I thank God.

TOUCHSTONE:

'Thank God.' A good answer.

Art rich?

WILLIAM:

Faith, sir, soso.

TOUCHSTONE:

'So so' is good, very good, very excellent good; and yet it is not; it is but soso. Art thou wise?

WILLIAM:

Ay, sir, I have a pretty wit.

TOUCHSTONE:

Why, thousay'st well. I do now remember a saying:

'The fool doth think he is wise, but the wise man knows himself to be a fool.' The heathen philosopher, when he had a desire to eat a grape, would open his lips when he put it into his mouth; meaning thereby that grapes were made to eat and lips to open. You do love this maid?

WILLIAM:

I do, sir.

TOUCHSTONE:

Give me your hand. Art thou learned?

WILLIAM:

No, sir.

TOUCHSTONE:

Then learn this of me: to have is to have; for it is a figure in rhetoric that drink, beingpour'd out of cup into a glass, by filling the one doth empty the other; for all your writers do consent that ipse is he; now, you are not ipse, for I am he.

WILLIAM:

Which he, sir?

TOUCHSTONE:

He, sir, that must marry this woman. Therefore, you clown, abandon- which is in the vulgar leave- the society-which in the boorish is company- of this female- which in the common is woman- which together is: abandon the society of this female; or, clown, thouperishest; or, to thy better understanding, diest; or, to wit, I kill thee, make thee away, translate thy life into death, thy liberty into bondage. I will deal in poison with thee, or in bastinado, or in steel; I will bandy with thee in faction; will o'er-run thee with policy; I will kill thee a hundred and fifty ways; therefore tremble and depart.

AUDREY:

Do, good William.

WILLIAM:

God rest you merry, sir.

[*Exit*]

[*Enter CORIN*]

CORIN:

Our master and mistress seeks you; come away, away.

TOUCHSTONE:

Trip, Audrey, trip, Audrey. I attend, I attend.

[*Exeunt*]

SCENE II.
The forest

[*Enter ORLANDO and OLIVER*]

ORLANDO:

Is't possible that on so little acquaintance you should like her? that but seeing you should love her? and loving woo? and, wooing, she should grant? and will youpersever to enjoy her?

OLIVER:

Neither call the giddiness of it in question, the poverty of her, the small acquaintance, my sudden wooing, nor her sudden consenting; but say with me, I loveAliena; say with her that she loves me; consent with both that we may enjoy each other. It shall be to your good; for my father's house and all the revenue that was old Sir Rowland's will I estate upon you, and here live and die a shepherd.

ORLANDO:

You have my consent. Let your wedding be to-morrow.
Thither will I invite the Duke and all's contented followers.
Go you and prepareAliena; for, look you, here comes my Rosalind.

[*Enter ROSALIND*]

ROSALIND:

God save you, brother.

OLIVER:

And you, fair sister.

[*Exit*]

ROSALIND:

O, my dear Orlando, how it grieves me to see thee wear thy heart in a scarf!

ORLANDO:

It is my arm.

ROSALIND:

I thought thy heart had been wounded with the claws of a lion.

ORLANDO:

Wounded it is, but with the eyes of a lady.

ROSALIND:

Did your brother tell you how I counterfeited to swoon when heshow'd me your handkercher?

ORLANDO:

Ay, and greater wonders than that.

ROSALIND:

O, I know where you are. Nay, 'tis true. There was never any thing so sudden but the fight of two rams and Caesar's thrasonical brag of 'I came, saw, and overcame.' For your brother and my sister no sooner met but theylook'd; no sooner look'd but theylov'd; no sooner lov'd but they sigh'd; no sooner sigh'd but theyask'd one another the reason; no sooner knew the reason but they sought the remedy- and in these degrees have they made pair of stairs to marriage, which they will climb incontinent, or else be incontinent before marriage. They are in the very wrath of love, and they will together. Clubs cannot part them.

ORLANDO:

They shall be married to-morrow; and I will bid the Duke to the nuptial. But, O, how bitter a thing it is to look into happiness through another man's eyes! By so much the more shall I to-morrow be at the height of heart-heaviness, by how much I shall think my brother happy in having what he wishes for.

ROSALIND:

Why, then, to-morrow I cannot serve your turn for Rosalind?

ORLANDO:

I can live no longer by thinking.

ROSALIND:

I will weary you, then, no longer with idle talking.
Know of me then- for now I speak to some purpose- that I know you are a gentleman of good conceit. I speak not this

that you should bear a good opinion of my knowledge, insomuch I say I know you are; neither do I labour for a greater esteem than may in some little measure draw a belief from you, to do yourself good, and not to grace me. Believe then, if you please, that I can do strange things. I have, since I was three year old, convers'd with a magician, most profound in his art and yet not damnable.

If you do love Rosalind so near the heart as your gesture cries it out, when your brother marries Aliena shall you marry her.

I know into what straits of fortune she is driven; and it is not impossible to me, if it appear not inconvenient to you, to set her before your eyes to-morrow, human as she is, and without any danger.

ORLANDO:

Speak'st thou in sober meanings?

ROSALIND:

By my life, I do; which I tender dearly, though I say I am a magician. Therefore put you in your best array, bid your friends; for if you will be married to-morrow, you shall; and to Rosalind, if you will.

[*Enter SILVIUS and PHEBE*]

Look, here comes a lover of mine, and a lover of hers.

PHEBE:

Youth, you have done me much ungentleness
To show the letter that I writ to you.

ROSALIND:

I care not if I have. It is my study
To seem despiteful and ungentle to you.
You are therefollow'd by a faithful shepherd;
Look upon him, love him; he worships you.

PHEBE:

Good shepherd, tell this youth what 'tis to love.

SILVIUS:

It is to be all made of sighs and tears;
And so am I for Phebe.

PHEBE:

And I for Ganymede.

ORLANDO:

And I for Rosalind.

ROSALIND:

And I for no woman.

SILVIUS:

It is to be all made of faith and service;

And so am I forPhebe.

PHEBE:

And I for Ganymede.

ORLANDO:

And I for Rosalind.

ROSALIND:

And I for no woman.

SILVIUS:

It is to be all made of fantasy,

All made of passion, and all made of wishes;

All adoration, duty, and observance,

All humbleness, all patience, and impatience,

All purity, all trial, all obedience;

And so am I forPhebe.

PHEBE:

And so am I for Ganymede.

ORLANDO:

And so am I for Rosalind.

ROSALIND:

And so am I for no woman.

PHEBE:

If this be so, why blame you me to love you?

SILVIUS:

If this be so, why blame you me to love you?

ORLANDO:

If this be so, why blame you me to love you?

ROSALIND:

Why do you speak too, 'Why blame you me to love you?'

ORLANDO:

To her that is not here, nor doth not hear.

ROSALIND:

Pray you, no more of this; 'tis like the howling of Irish wolves against the moon. [To SILVIUS] I will help you if I can. [*To PHEBE*] I would love you if I could. - To-morrow meet me all together. [*To PHEBE*] I will marry you if ever I marry woman, and I'll be married to-morrow. [To ORLANDO] I will satisfy you if ever I satisfied man, and you shall be married to-morrow. [*To Silvius*] I will content you if what pleases you contents you, and you shall be married to-morrow. [*To ORLANDO*] As you love Rosalind, meet. [*To SILVIUS*] As you lovePhebe, meet;- and as I love no woman, I'll meet. So, fare you well; I have left you commands.

SILVIUS:

I'll not fail, if I live.

PHEBE:

Nor I.

ORLANDO:

Nor I.

[*Exeunt*]

SCENE III.
The forest

[*Enter TOUCHSTONE and AUDREY*]

TOUCHSTONE:

To-morrow is the joyful day, Audre'y; to-morrow will we be married.

AUDREY:

I do desire it with all my heart; and I hope it is no dishonest desire to desire to be a woman of the world. Here come two of thebanish'd Duke's pages.

[*Enter two PAGES*]

FIRST PAGE:

Well met, honest gentleman.

TOUCHSTONE:

By my troth, well met. Come sit, sit, and a song.

SECOND PAGE:

We are for you; siti' th' middle.

FIRST PAGE:

Shall we clapinto't roundly, without hawking, or spitting, or saying we are hoarse, which are the only prologues to a bad voice?

SECOND PAGE:

I'faith, i'faith; and both in a tune, like two gipsies on a horse.

[*SONG.*]

It was a lover and his lass,
With a hey, and a ho, and a heynonino,
That o'er the green corn-field did pass
In the spring time, the only pretty ring time,
When birds do sing, hey ding a ding, ding.
Sweet lovers love the spring.
Between the acres of the rye,
With a hey, and a ho, and a heynonino,

These pretty country folks would lie,

In the spring time, &c.

This carol they began that hour,

With a hey, and a ho, and a heynonino,

How that a life was but a flower,

In the spring time, &c.

And therefore take the present time,

With a hey, and a ho, and a heynonino,

For love is crowned with the prime,

In the spring time, &c.

TOUCHSTONE:

Truly, young gentlemen, though there was no great matter in the ditty, yet the note was veryuntuneable.

FIRST PAGE:

YOU are deceiv'd, sir; we kept time, we lost not our time.

TOUCHSTONE:

By my troth, yes; I count it but time lost to hear such a foolish song. God buy you; and God mend your voices. Come, Audrey.

[*Exeunt*]

SCENE IV.
The forest

[*Enter DUKE SENIOR, AMIENS, JAQUES, ORLANDO, OLI-VER, and CELIA*]

DUKE SENIOR:

Dost thou believe, Orlando, that the boy Can do all this that he hath promised?

ORLANDO:

I sometimes do believe and sometimes do not:
As those that fear they hope, and know they fear.

[*Enter ROSALIND, SILVIUS, and PHEBE*]

ROSALIND:

Patience once more, whiles our compact isurg'd:
You say, if I bring in your Rosalind,
You will bestow her on Orlando here?

DUKE SENIOR:

That would I, had I kingdoms to give with her.

ROSALIND:

And you say you will have her when I bring her?

ORLANDO:

That would I, were I of all kingdoms king.

ROSALIND:

You say you'll marry me, if I be willing?

PHEBE:

That will I, should I die the hour after.

ROSALIND:

But if you do refuse to marry me,

You'll give yourself to this most faithful shepherd?

PHEBE:

So is the bargain.

ROSALIND:

You say that you'll have Phebe, if she will?

SILVIUS:

Though to have her and death were both one thing.

ROSALIND:

I have promis'd to make all this matter even.

Keep you your word, O Duke, to give your daughter;

You yours, Orlando, to receive his daughter;

Keep your word, Phebe, that you'll marry me,

Or else, refusing me, to wed this shepherd;

Keep your word, Silvius, that you'll marry her
If she refuse me; and from hence I go,
To make these doubts all even.

[*Exeunt ROSALIND and CELIA*]

DUKE SENIOR:

I do remember in this shepherd boy
Some lively touches of my daughter'sfavour.

ORLANDO:

My lord, the first time that I ever saw him
Methought he was a brother to your daughter.
But, my good lord, this boy is forest-born,
And hath beentutor'd in the rudiments
Of many desperate studies by his uncle,
Whom he reports to be a great magician,
Obscured in the circle of this forest.

[*Enter TOUCHSTONE and AUDREY*]

JAQUES:

There is, sure, another flood toward, and these couples are coming to the ark. Here comes a pair of very strange beasts

which in all tongues arecall'd fools.
TOUCHSTONE:
Salutation and greeting to you all!
JAQUES:
Good my lord, bid him welcome. This is the motley-minded gentleman that I have so often met in the forest. He hath been a courtier, he swears.
TOUCHSTONE:
If any man doubt that, let him put me to my purgation. I have trod a measure; I haveflatt'red a lady; I have been politic with my friend, smooth with mine enemy; I have undone three tailors; I have had four quarrels, and like to have fought one.
JAQUES:
And how was thatta'en up?
TOUCHSTONE:
Faith, we met, and found the quarrel was upon the seventh cause.
JAQUES:
How seventh cause? Good my lord, like this fellow.
DUKE SENIOR:
I like him very well.
TOUCHSTONE:

God 'ild you, sir; I desire you of the like. I press in here, sir, amongst the rest of the country copulatives, to swear and to forswear, according as marriage binds and blood breaks. A poor virgin, sir, an ill-favour'd thing, sir, but mine own; a poorhumour of mine, sir, to take that that man else will.
Rich honesty dwells like a miser, sir, in a poor house; as your pearl in your foul oyster.

DUKE SENIOR:

By my faith, he is very swift and sententious.

TOUCHSTONE:

According to the fool's bolt, sir, and such dulcet diseases.

JAQUES:

But, for the seventh cause: how did you find the quarrel on the seventh cause?

TOUCHSTONE:

Upon a lie seven times removed- bear your body more seeming, Audrey- as thus, sir. I did dislike the cut of a certain courtier's beard; he sent me word, if I said his beard was not cut well, he was in the mind it was. This iscall'd the Retort Courteous. If I sent him word again it was not well cut, he would send me word he cut it to please himself. This iscall'd the Quip Modest. If again it was not well cut, he disabled my judgment.

This is call'd the Reply Churlish. If again it was not well cut, he would answer I spake not true. This is call'd the Reproof Valiant. If again it was not well cut, he would say I lie. This is call'd the Countercheck Quarrelsome. And so to the Lie Circumstantial and the Lie Direct.

JAQUES:

And how oft did you say his beard was not well cut?

TOUCHSTONE:

I durst go no further than the Lie Circumstantial, nor he durst not give me the Lie Direct; and so we measur'd swords and parted.

JAQUES:

Can you nominate in order now the degrees of the lie?

TOUCHSTONE:

O, sir, we quarrel in print by the book, as you have books for good manners. I will name you the degrees. The first, the Retort Courteous; the second, the Quip Modest; the third, the Reply Churlish; the fourth, the Reproof Valiant; the fifth, the Countercheck Quarrelsome; the sixth, the Lie with Circumstance; the seventh, the Lie Direct. All these you may avoid but the Lie Direct; and you may avoid that too with an If. I knew when seven justices could not take up a quarrel; but when the parties were met themselves, one of them thought but of an If, as: 'If you said so, then I said so.' And they shook hands, and swore brothers. Your If is the only peace-maker; much virtue in If.

JAQUES:

Is not this a rare fellow, my lord?

He's as good atany thing, and yet a fool.

DUKE SENIOR:

He uses his folly like a stalking-horse, and under the presentation of that he shoots his wit:

[*Enter HYMEN, ROSALIND, and CELIA. Still MUSIC*]

HYMEN:

Then is there mirth in heaven,

When earthly things made even

Atone together.

Good Duke, receive thy daughter;

Hymen from heaven brought her,

Yea, brought her hither,

That thoumightst join her hand with his,

Whose heart within his bosom is.

ROSALIND:

[*To DUKE*] To you I give myself, for I am yours.

[*To ORLANDO*] To you I give myself, for I am yours.

DUKE SENIOR:

If there be truth in sight, you are my daughter.

ORLANDO:

If there be truth in sight, you are my Rosalind.

PHEBE:

If sight and shape be true,

Why then, my love adieu!

ROSALIND:

I'll have no father, if you be not he;

I'll have no husband, if you be not he;

Nor ne'er wed woman, if you be not she.

HYMEN:

Peace, ho! I bar confusion;

'Tis I must make conclusion

Of these most strange events.

Here's eight that must take hands

To join in Hymen's bands,

If truth holds true contents.

You and you no cross shall part;

You and you are heart in heart;

You to his love must accord,

Or have a woman to your lord;

You and you are sure together,
As the winter to foul weather.
Whiles a wedlock-hymn we sing,
Feed yourselves with questioning,
That reason wonder may diminish,
How thus we met, and these things finish.

[*SONG*]

Wedding is great Juno's crown;
O blessed bond of board and bed!
'Tis Hymen peoples every town;
High wedlock then behonoured.
Honour, high honour, and renown,
To Hymen, god of every town!

DUKE SENIOR:

O my dear niece, welcome thou art to me!
Even daughter, welcome in no less degree.

PHEBE:

I will not eat my word, now thou art mine;
Thy faith my fancy to thee doth combine.

[*Enter JAQUES de BOYS*]

JAQUES de BOYS:

> Let me have audience for a word or two.
> I am the second son of old Sir Rowland,
> That bring these tidings to this fair assembly.
> Duke Frederick, hearing how that every day
> Men of great worth resorted to this forest,
> Address'd a mighty power; which were on foot,
> In his own conduct, purposely to take
> His brother here, and put him to the sword;
> And to the skirts of this wild wood he came,
> Where, meeting with an old religious man,
> After some question with him, was converted
> Both from his enterprise and from the world;
> His crown bequeathing to hisbanish'd brother,
> And all their landsrestor'd to them again
> That were with himexil'd. This to be true
> I do engage my life.

DUKE SENIOR:

> Welcome, young man.
> Thouoffer'st fairly to thy brothers' wedding:
> To one, his lands withheld; and to the other,
> A land itself at large, a potent dukedom.

First, in this forest let us do those ends
That here were well begun and well begot;
And after, every of this happy number,
That haveendur'd shrewd days and nights with us,
Shall share the good of our returned fortune,
According to the measure of their states.
Meantime, forget this new-fall'n dignity,
And fall into our rustic revelry.
Play, music; and you brides and bridegrooms all,
With measureheap'd in joy, to th' measures fall.

JAQUES:

Sir, by your patience. If I heard you rightly,
The Duke hath put on a religious life,
And thrown into neglect the pompous court.

JAQUES DE BOYS:

He hath.

JAQUES:

To him will I. Out of theseconvertites
There is much matter to be heard andlearn'd.
[*To DUKE*] You to your formerhonour I bequeath;
Your patience and your virtue well deserves it.
[*To ORLANDO*] You to a love that your true faith doth merit;

[*To OLIVER*] You to your land, and love, and great allies
[*To SILVIUS*] You to a long and well-deserved bed;
[*To TOUCHSTONE*] And you to wrangling; for thy loving voyage
Is but for two monthsvictuall'd. - So to your pleasures;
I am for other than for dancing measures.

DUKE SENIOR:
Stay, Jaques, stay.

JAQUES:
To see no pastime I. What you would have
I'll stay to know at yourabandon'd cave.

[*Exit*]

DUKE SENIOR:
Proceed, proceed. We will begin these rites,
As we do trust they'll end, in true delights. [*A dance*]

[*Exeunt*]

EPILOGUE and ROSALIND:
It is not the fashion to see the lady the epilogue; but it is no more unhandsome than to see the lord the prologue. If it be

true that good wine needs no bush, 'tis true that a good play needs no epilogue. Yet to good wine they do use good bushes; and good plays prove the better by the help of good epilogues.

What a case am I in then, that am neither a good epilogue, nor cannot insinuate with you in the behalf of a good play! I am not furnish'd like a beggar; therefore to beg will not become me.

My way is to conjure you; and I'll begin with the women. I charge you, O women, for the love you bear to men, to like as much of this play as please you; and I charge you, O men, for the love you bear to women- as I perceive by your simp'ring none of you hates them- that between you and the women the play may please.

If I were a woman, I would kiss as many of you as had beards that pleas'd me, complexions that lik'd me, and breaths that I defied not; and, I am sure, as many as have good beards, or good faces, or sweet breaths, will, for my kind offer, when I make curtsy, bid me farewell.

[*Exeunt*]